SERVICE WITH A SMILE

by Bert Cranthorne

Published by New Generation Publishing in 2012

www.newgeneration-publishing.com

 **New Generation Publishing**

Cartoons covering early service were drawn to occupy my time during the long sea voyage from England to South Africa in 1942. Maurice, a fellow trainee navigator, who had been a draughtsman, added text in pencil to accompany my drawings. When we finished our course he managed to get photocopies printed and when we parted company and returned to England I gave him the sketch book and kept the copies for use when I arrived back home.

I continued drawing cartoons and sketches (some in watercolour) during training and operational service.

Everything became very faded and discoloured due to the poor quality of wartime paper. I have now been able to restore my work on computer and then complete *Service with a Smile.*

B.C.

CONTENTS

CHAPTER ONE

BETWEEN THE WARS

I CAME INTO the world some twenty-nine months after the 1914-1918 Great War - "A war to end all wars!"

As a boy in the nineteen twenties I was able to marvel at such new wonders of science and technology as 'crystal and catswhisker' wireless sets with headphones, black and white silent movies, gramophones, gas lighting both indoors and in the street, and portable roll-film box cameras   In the thirties, during my time at Central School, advances were made in the development of loudspeaker radios, powered by wet and dry batteries, able to receive broadcasts from France and Holland. There was also a wonderful new invention featuring a revolving disk with a spiral of thirty holes which was able to transmit and receive pictures by wireless over short distances and called "Television" by its inventor John Logie Baird.

.

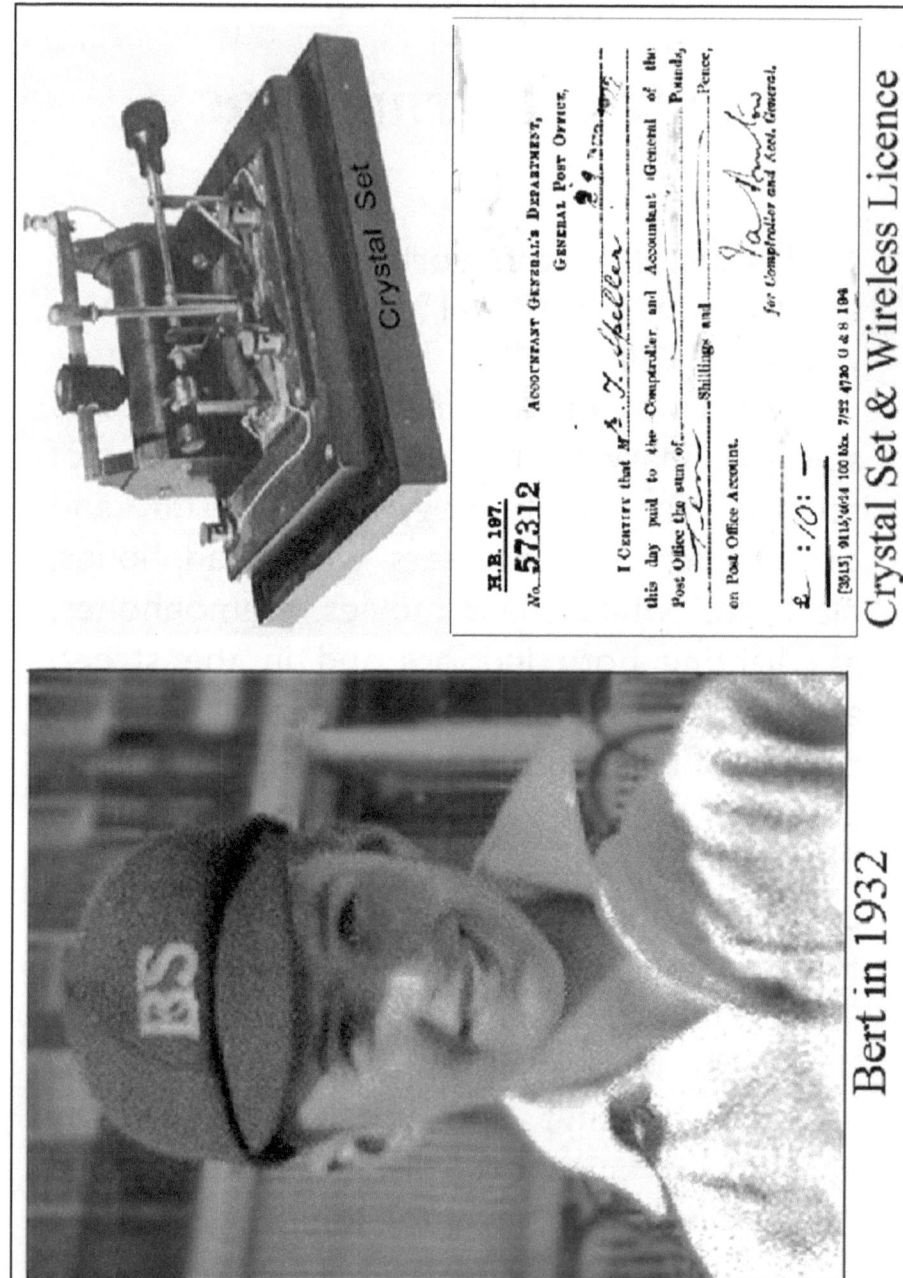

Crystal Set

Bert in 1932

Crystal Set & Wireless Licence

By the middle of the thirties I was made aware of the Third Reich by my collection of foreign postage stamps over-printed with new prices in millions of German Marks!   At school we were paid a visit by a group of German students who, when leaving our classroom, threw their right arms aloft yelling "Heil Hitler!" My School Certificates were successfully obtained in 1937 and with my academic course finally completed, I left school at Easter 1938.

Jobs were scarce and the Central Schools' Employment Bureau at Snow Hill in the City of London could only offer a choice of vacancies with the London & North-Eastern Railway Company or H.M. Forces. Following interviews at the City Office of the former, I started work on 25th April as a junior clerk on £55 per annum. I was transferred to the Chief Office of the Railway Police in Pindar Street, close to Liverpool Street Station, for £90 per annum, and on 26th June 1939 was appointed to the permanent staff.

During these early months of my working career, the rumblings of war were in the air, and the newspapers were reporting that Austria had been taken over and absorbed into the new German Reich and we were being given instruction and various booklets on air raid precautions. We all gave a sigh of relief when the Prime Minister Neville Chamberlain flew to Germany for meetings with Herr Hitler and obtained the famous "Peace in our time!" agreement, but the World watched as Germany marched into Czecho-Slovakia to "protect" German interests in the Sudetenland.

This was followed by new demands that "Danzig, the Polish Corridor, must be returned to the Reich!" A **Russo-German non-aggression Agreement** and an **Anglo-Polish Mutual Assistance** Pact were signed during August but to our dismay, at the end of the month, Herr Hitler, the German Chancellor demanded incorporation of Poland into Greater Germany.

On 3rd September 1939, following the invasion of Poland by German troops, Neville Chamberlain made the fateful radio broadcast.

The Thames off Greenwich, 1937

:London 1937

TERMS AND CONDITIONS
UPON WHICH CANDIDATES ARE ADMITTED INTO THE SERVICE OF
THE
LONDON AND NORTH EASTERN RAILWAY COMPANY
AS CLERKS

The Company are prepared to accept as Clerks a limited number of young men who have passed either an examination of University Matriculation standard or who have obtained the School Certificate. Entrance to the Company's service is also open to youths who are neither of Matriculation standard, nor have been awarded the School Certificate, but in such cases candidates will be required to sit a written examination and to satisfy the Examiners in the Company's prescribed tests in educational subjects. In every case, however, candidates will be required to satisfy a Committee of the Company's Officers at a personal interview before appointment to the service and to pass a medical examination by the Company's Medical Officer as to physical fitness, including eyesight.

Each candidate must send in a formal application in his own handwriting giving full personal particulars in the form attached hereto. He must also furnish a certificate of birth, a certificate of health from a qualified medical man and two testimonials as to character, one of which must be from the Master of the School he last attended, and the other from some responsible person.

Applicants must normally be not more than 18 years of age, though candidates of slightly higher age may be accepted, provided that they have special qualifications. Successful candidates will be regarded as Probationary Clerks for the first twelve months, their permanent appointment to the service being dependent upon a satisfactory report from the Company's Officers at the end of that period.

Appointments are made on the distinct understanding that applicants are prepared to conform with the following terms and conditions :—

1. Every clerk must make himself acquainted with the Company's Rules and Regulations.

2. Every Clerk must be prepared to take duty at whatever place the Company may desire him to do so.

3. The Company may also require any Clerk to become proficient in shorthand within a reasonable time of his entering the service.

4. Every Clerk must, when required by the Company to do so, become a member of and comply with the rules of the Company's Superannuation Fund, and the amounts of his subscriptions or contributions thereto will be deducted from his salary.

5. If a Clerk does not conduct himself satisfactorily, or it is found he is not qualified for the Company's service, the Company may at any time dispense with his services. One week's notice will be given to, or required from, Clerks previous to their leaving the Company's service. In the event of any Clerk leaving without giving such notice, any pay due to him will be forfeited.

6. The Company reserve the right to dismiss without notice or to suspend from duty and after enquiry dismiss any Clerk for intoxication, disobedience of orders, negligence or misconduct, or for being absent from duty without leave, and to withold permanently the salary which would have been earned by any Clerk, during the time of such suspension or during his absence from duty.

7. The present scale of salaries for Clerks is as follows :—

Age in Years.			Junior Class					Per Annum.
								£
15	...	...	...	...	...	...	...	35
16	...	...	...	...	...	...	...	45
17	...	...	...	...	...	...	...	55

At Hadley Wood 1941

Wartime Booklet

The PM's message

The broadcast given on the morning of 3 September 1939, in which the Rt Hon Neville Chamberlain announced that Britain was at war with Germany

I AM speaking to you from the Cabinet Room at 10 Downing Street. This morning the British Ambassador in Berlin handed the German Government a final note stating that, unless we heard from them by 11 o'clock that they were prepared at once to withdraw their troops from Poland, a state of war would exist between us. I have to tell you now that no such undertaking has been received, and that consequently this country is at war with Germany.

You can imagine what a bitter blow it is to me that all my long struggle to win peace has failed. Yet I cannot believe that there is anything more or anything different that I could have done and that would have been more successful.

Up to the very last it would have been quite possible to have arranged a peaceful and honourable settlement between Germany and Poland, but Hitler would not have it. He had evidently made up his mind to attack Poland whatever happened, and although he now says he put forward reasonable proposals which were rejected by the Poles, that is not a true statement.

The proposals were never shown to the Poles, nor to us, and, though they were announced in a German broadcast on Thursday night, Hitler did not wait to hear comments on them, but ordered his troops to cross the Polish frontier. His action shows convincingly that there is no chance of expecting that this man will ever give up his practice of using force to gain his will. He can only be stopped by force.

We and France are today, in fulfilment of our obligations, going to the aid of Poland, who is so bravely resisting this wicked and unprovoked attack on her people. We have a clear conscience. We have done all that any country could do to establish peace. The situation in which no word given by Germany's ruler could be trusted, and no people or country could feel themselves safe, has become intolerable. And now that we have resolved to finish it, I know that you will all play your part with calmness and courage.

At such a moment as this, the assurances of support that we have received from the Empire are a source of profound encouragement to us.

When I have finished speaking, certain detailed announcements will be made on behalf of the Government. Give these your closest attention. The Government have made plans under which it will be possible to carry on the work of the nation in the days of stress and strain that may be ahead. But these plans need your help.

You may be taking your part in the fighting services or as a volunteer in one of the branches of Civil Defence. If so you will report for duty in accordance with the instructions you have received. You may be engaged in work essential to the prosecution of war for the maintenance of the life of the people – in factories, in transport, in public utility concerns, or in the supply of other necessaries of life. If so, it is of vital importance that you should carry on with your jobs.

Now may God bless you all. May He defend the right. It is the evil things that we shall be fighting against – brute force, bad faith, injustice, oppression and persecution – and against them I am certain that the right will prevail.

CHAPTER TWO

THE HOME FRONT

THE RAILWAY POLICE OFFICE evacuated from the City of London to the Waiting Rooms on the platforms of New Barnet station and later moved into a requisitioned property at Hadley Wood.

We were still in the glorious days of steam trains, but now all carriage windows were blacked out with blinds and a border of black paint was put on the glass. The carriage lighting was reduced to a glimmer for travel at night during "black-out".

Commuting to and from work at this time was never without a dull moment! In the mornings I caught the train from Eltham Park station to London Bridge, then travelled by tube to King's Cross station, and finally by steam train to Hadley Wood.   In the evenings the same journeys were made in the reverse direction. On many evenings the air-raid siren began wailing when I was only halfway home and the platforms on the Tube stations were soon transformed into one huge air-raid shelter, with Londoners spreading out and settling down on makeshift bedding for the night, and leaving just enough space at the platform edge for passengers to board a train.

My walk home from Eltham Park station was always executed in record time. The sound of the enemy bombers, anti-aircraft gunfire and the "ping" and sparks made by shrapnel hitting the road spurred me on!

In the summer and autumn of 1940, the daytime skies were filled with vapour trails made by dogfighting aircraft, and the night skies were criss-crossed by searchlight beams and dotted with bursting anti-aircraft shells, and London was subjected to seventy-five consecutive nights of bombing by the Luftwaffe. The great fire in the City of London in May 1941 turned the sky into a huge flickering orange glow clearly visible from my home at Eltham..

In the early summer of 1941 I reported for a medical and interview for Military Service and by this time I was determined to volunteer for Aircrew duties - to be at the delivery, instead of the receiving end, of bombs.

My appointment for the stringent aircrew medical examination and interview at Euston House was scheduled for 8th August 1941. The Chief Clerk at the Police Office did not appear to be overwhelmed with joy at my decision to volunteer for service with R.A.F. aircrew, but granted me leave to attend provided that I made up the time in my lunch hours!   It was lunchtime sandwiches at my desk for the following week.

At Euston House I was moved around and inspected by a succession of medical experts who examined every part of my body in great detail.   Finally I was passed fit for all grades of aircrew and, following an interview by a board of examiners, I expressed as my first choice for aircrew duty, the position of Observer (Navigator\Bomb-aimer) in view of my interest and ability in mathematics.

So began my effort to change the course of the war! and on 10th November 1941 I reported to the Air Crew Reception Centre (No.1 A.C.R.C.) at Lords' Cricket Ground, St.John's Wood in London.

NAZIS BOMB FOUR EIRE VILLAGES: BACK PAGE

H-P SAUCE IMPROVES TASTE STOPS WASTE

Daily Sketch

LONDON AREA BOMBED IN ALL-NIGHT RAID

Six-Hour Alarm

TO BE GIVEN TO YOUR MEDICAL OFFICER

ON ARRIVAL AT YOUR FIRST R.A.F. Room 56

Naval Form M 252

EUSTON HOUSE.

Findings of Medical Board held at_____

_____

CRANTHORNE   ALBERT   HENRY

was medically   examined on___8 AUG 1941___ as to his fitness

for   AIR CREW DUTIES

and has been found to be—

(A) Fit_____

(B) Unfit_____

Reason for unfitness_____

_____

(c) Temporarily unfit_____

Reason for temporary unfitness_____

_____

Date (if any) applicant should report for re-examination

_____FIT_____

Remarks :—   PILOT   FITR/OBS A
              OBSERVER
              W/OPERATOR
              A/GUNNER
              Signature_____

President of Board or Competent
Medical Authority.

Fighting Fit!

CHAPTER THREE

RECEPTION

WE arrived at No.1 A.C.R.C.(Air-Crew Reception Centre), in Lords' cricket ground, from all parts of the United Kingdom, and soon began to realise that we were no longer regarded as individuals but 'numbers', and, following a request to take off all our clothes, were given our first inspection (F.F.I.) to certify that we were 'Free from infection'. Following a large amount of form filling, we were eventually allocated our "Flight" letter and marched to our various billets, which for me, turned out to be Viceroy Court.

The restaurant of the Regent's Park Zoo had been taken over as an R.A.F. cookhouse and provided us with our first meal before we were marched to the Stores to collect our new clothing or kit. Kitting was performed at an unbelievable speed with items thrown across a counter to be caught and gathered up and taken back to our billets.

"Lep roi, lep roi !" shouted the corporal as we marched along trying to keep all our kit intact.

It was wonderful to get into a bath and soak off all our dirt and sweat, but the next morning, the soiled baths, mirrors and chrome fittings had to be cleaned and polished and brought back to immaculate showroom condition ready for inspection!

The meal parades were a real test of organisation in order to get all the various Flights in and out of the Zoo restaurant at the scheduled time. To achieve this we were paraded at least half an hour before our allotted meal time, ready to march the half-mile or so to Regent's Park at the regulation pace of 140 steps to the minute.

Further medical checks were carried out at A.C.R.C. including x-rays, inoculation and vaccination of new entrants. Over the doorway of Abbey Lodge medical centre was the inscription "Abandon hope all ye who enter here!" Inside we queued to be injected with various vaccines and, those who were unfortunate enough to faint had their injections completed where they lay, on the floor!

Our days consisted of drill and P.T., various ability tests together with cleaning bathrooms and arranging beds and bedding. Guard duties were carried out during the freezing weather with a baton as our only armament. There was, of course, the inevitable corporal seeking volunteers for jobs, and on one occasion a knowledge of Shorthand was required! As one of a number of gullible volunteers I found to my cost that "They are 'short-handed' down at the cookhouse!" and wanted hands to peel potatoes!

On New Year's eve we were required to pack our bags ready to be taken to Victoria station to board a train for Brighton where we were to begin the next stage of our training which would include an introduction to Morse Code signalling.

Bringing our new kit back from the Stores

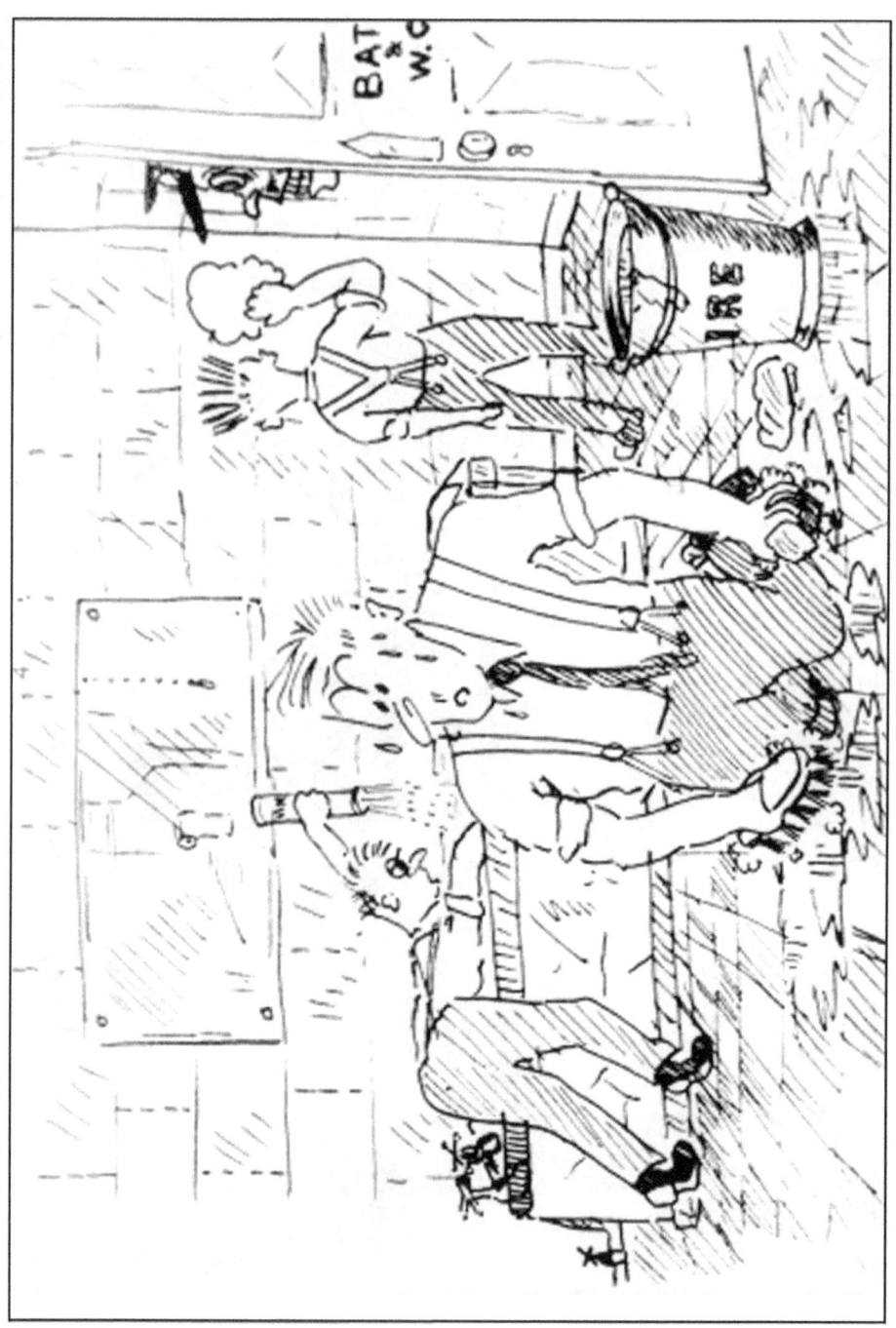

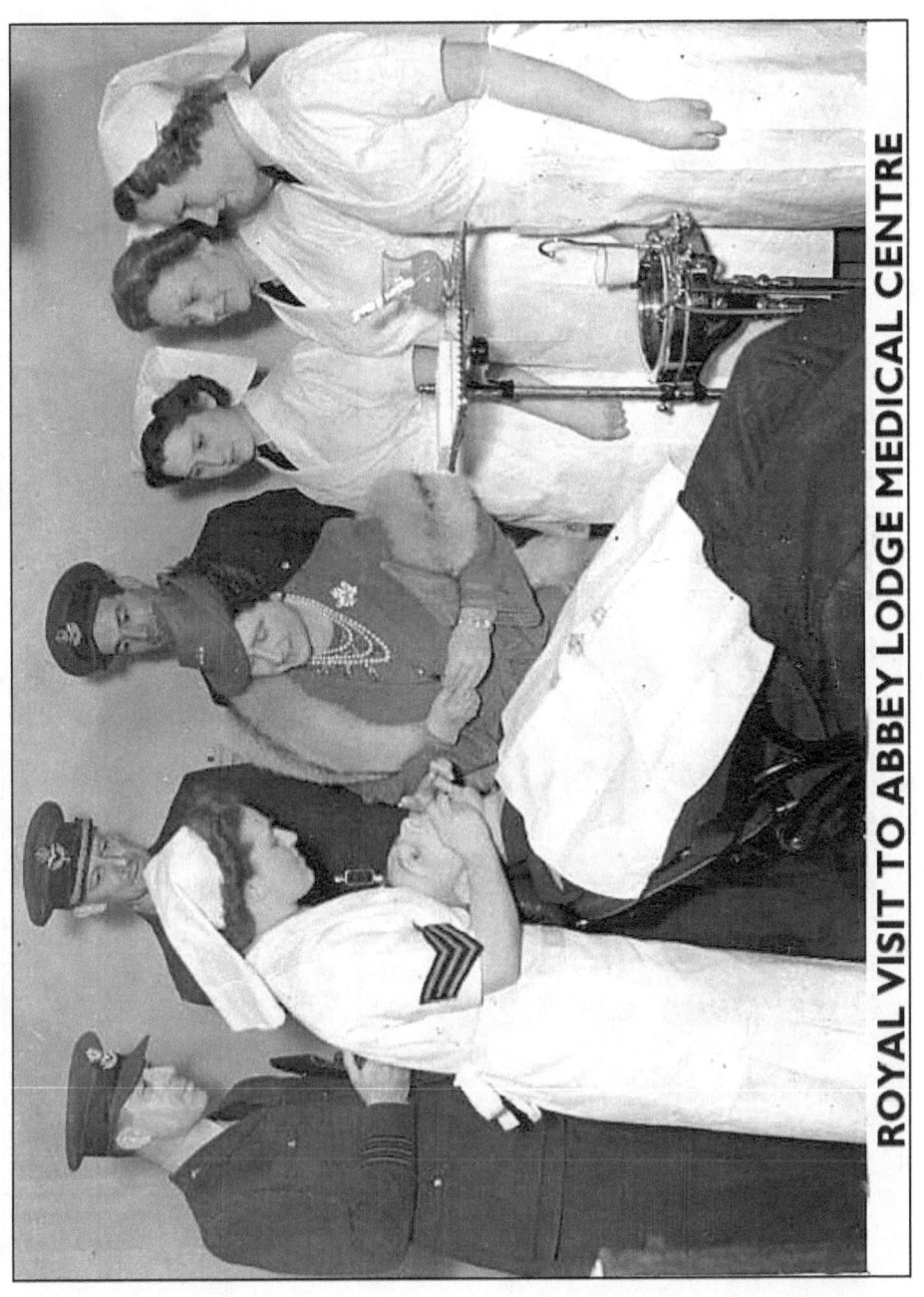

ROYAL VISIT TO ABBEY LODGE MEDICAL CENTRE

INTERNATIONAL MORSE CODE

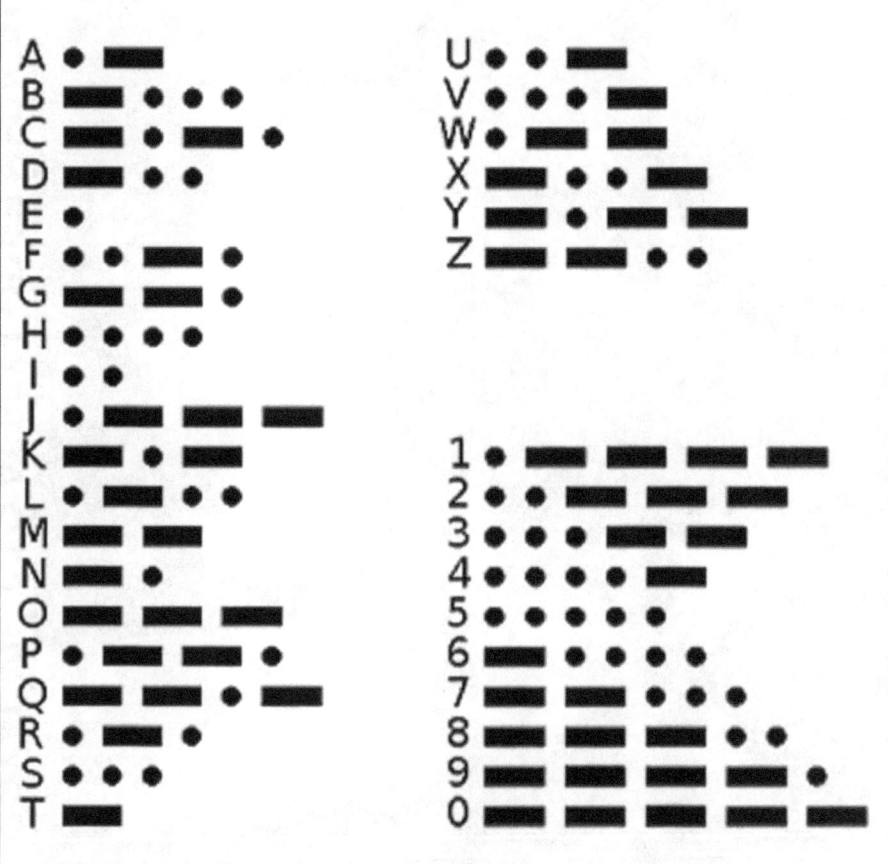

CHAPTER FOUR

DISPOSAL

WE marched from Brighton railway station pondering over the title of our new home at A.C.D.W. (Aircrew Disposal Wing). The Grand Hotel had been taken over by the R.A.F. but had been stripped of most of it's interior furniture and fittings, but had an abundance of dust on the bare floorboards and mature tide-marks and dirty metalwork in the bathrooms. Our ability as cleaners must have gone on ahead of us because we were put to work at once with our mops and polishes. Before cleaning up however, the all-important F.F.I. examination had to be undertaken. Our long row of naked bodies was scanned by the medical officer, who used an electric torch to illuminate his prey!

The importance of fresh air was impressed upon us and this was, in fact, backed up by official orders. Windows and doors had to be kept open by day and night and the January weather with biting winds, snow and ice ensured that we kept on the move.

At night we slept with our clothes on and supplemented the blankets with a greatcoat. Evenings found the building interior bathed in a ghostly blue light as the light-bulbs were painted blue during "blackout". At mealtimes, the seven-storey staircase of the Grand was filled with a long queue of airmen carrying metal dinner plates, mugs and "irons", patiently moving slowly downward. The cookhouse always welcomed volunteers for washing-up and potato peeling, and these were provided, in part, after the daily inspection of beds, when our folded blankets were checked to see whether the prescribed two inches was adhered to! We were given daily instruction in Aircraft Recognition, Anti-Gas Drill, Mathematics and Signals. Civilian Instructors were employed to teach us the Morse Code up to a speed of four words a minute. After successfully completing our examinations, we awaited our next move, and on 24th January we left Brighton station on a night train and dozed on our way to I.T.W. (Initial Training Wing)..

'Freeze a jolly good fellow'

'Wrong again! Take that man's name'

CHAPTER FIVE

INITIAL TRAINING

We arrived in Torquay at an early hour and were greeted by warm breezes, green lawns and gardens with palms, which seemed unbelievable after the cold and unwelcome climate we left behind us at Brighton. The accommodation also offered the same contrast, with clean rooms equipped with lockers for storage of our kit. We enjoyed a good breakfast in a bright and inviting dining hall.

Following the usual form filling preceded by a welcoming address we were taken outside and given our first drill instruction by a corporal who, we understood, was an ex trapeze artist. We were shown how to parade in I.T.W. fashion with the comment "I am da great Sabate! Brace op -- morve you pipporl!" He demonstrated his drill movements which we attempted to copy. Subsequently our boots were fitted with metal studs to ensure that all movements were strictly synchronised.

Our fitness improved noticeably and cross-country runs to the village of Cockington were a real test of this. On the daily parade, the white "flash" added to our caps was expected to be "snow white", our tunic buttons sparkling clean, our trousers properly creased and our boots polished to a mirror like finish.

Lectures were given at various locations around the town and we marched to these at the regulation 140 paces to the minute, with arms swinging to shoulder height, in spite of the very steep upward slope of the roads. Our instructor in Mathematics and Navigation seemed to have a permanently furrowed brow as he struggled to teach us the fundamentals of these subjects. Any errors made by us were greeted by the comment "No no no rubbish! - Don't do it my way! - it might help you!"

Instruction was also given in the stripping and reassembly of the Vickers Gas Operated machine gun and, at the same venue, instruction was given to increase our speed in sending and receiving messages by Morse code.

We were introduced to signalling by Aldis lamp and practice in this took place between two high points in Torquay. On these occasions the weather was usually bad and if we complained of difficulty in reading the distant blinking light through eyes watering with the cold, we were told not to expect a young searchlight!

The rest of our stay at I.T.W. was taken up with intensive swotting, physical training and parades through the town. At last we sat for the examinations, and after the completion of these, we received an unexpected surprise -- our first home leave, on 2nd April!

On return from leave we were relieved and surprised to learn that we had all passed the exams and given promotion to L.A.C. (Leading Aircraftman). A few hours later we learned that we were leaving Torquay to travel overnight --- we hardly had sufficient time to sew on our L.A.C. "Props".

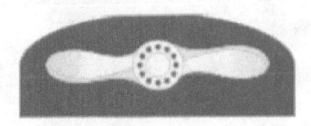

I.T.W. Torquay
Aircrew Cadets 1942

Keeping fit at I.T.W. Torquay

"You can't expect a young searchlight!"

Bert 1942

CHAPTER 6

GETTING DOWN TO BUSINESS

WARTIME Eastbourne was the temporary home of the RAF Elementary Air Navigation School (E.A.N.S.) and it was here that we would get down to the serious business of learning how to navigate.

Soon after settling in our rooms at the usual seafront hotel, our kit was inspected, or rather, casually examined, by our new Flight commander. His genial manner and flow of ripe language during this inspection, was in extreme contrast to our previous experience at training stations. We also noticed that he was wearing an aircrew brevet, and we later found that all E.A.N.S., instructors were fully qualified flyers.

Our new tutors spent the first few days trying to ascertain how much (or little) that we had learned at I.T.W. It was soon evident that much additional evening study would be necessary, and our daily work had to be supplemented by wading through the R.A.F. Navigation Manual AP 1234.

We were also introduced to an ingenious mechanical circular slide rule cum plotting tool known as the Dalton Computer. This enabled us to complete laborious I.T.W. style air-plots in a matter of minutes. We subsequently discovered that the examination standard air-plots at E.A.N.S., would take a couple of hours even when using this new mechanical aid.

Our physical fitness still featured as an important part of the curriculum. P.T. sessions took place on the lower paved area of the promenade, and provided entertainment for local residents passing by at street level above. A medical examination to check on our fitness included the customary blowing a column of mercury up a graduated tube and holding it there for a specified time until our lungs felt like exploding.

Eastbourne was subjected to many enemy hit-and-run air raids during our stay. Raiding aircraft raked the sea front with cannon fire and dropped the occasional bomb.

When this occurred during lectures, we dropped to the floor at the sound of the gunfire, waiting for the bomb explosion. When our billets were damaged during one of these raids, we were allowed to return for a brief visit to collect our small kit, after which we were moved to another building nearby.

Several nights were spent sleeping on the floor of our temporary quarters until repairs had been carried out. The increased frequency of these attacks resulted in the setting up of a "station defence". The anti-aircraft arrangements for this meant that of one of us would have to sit behind a V.G.O. machine gun on top of a local building watching for enemy aircraft, and hoping to either scare it off, or even more unlikely, shoot it down!

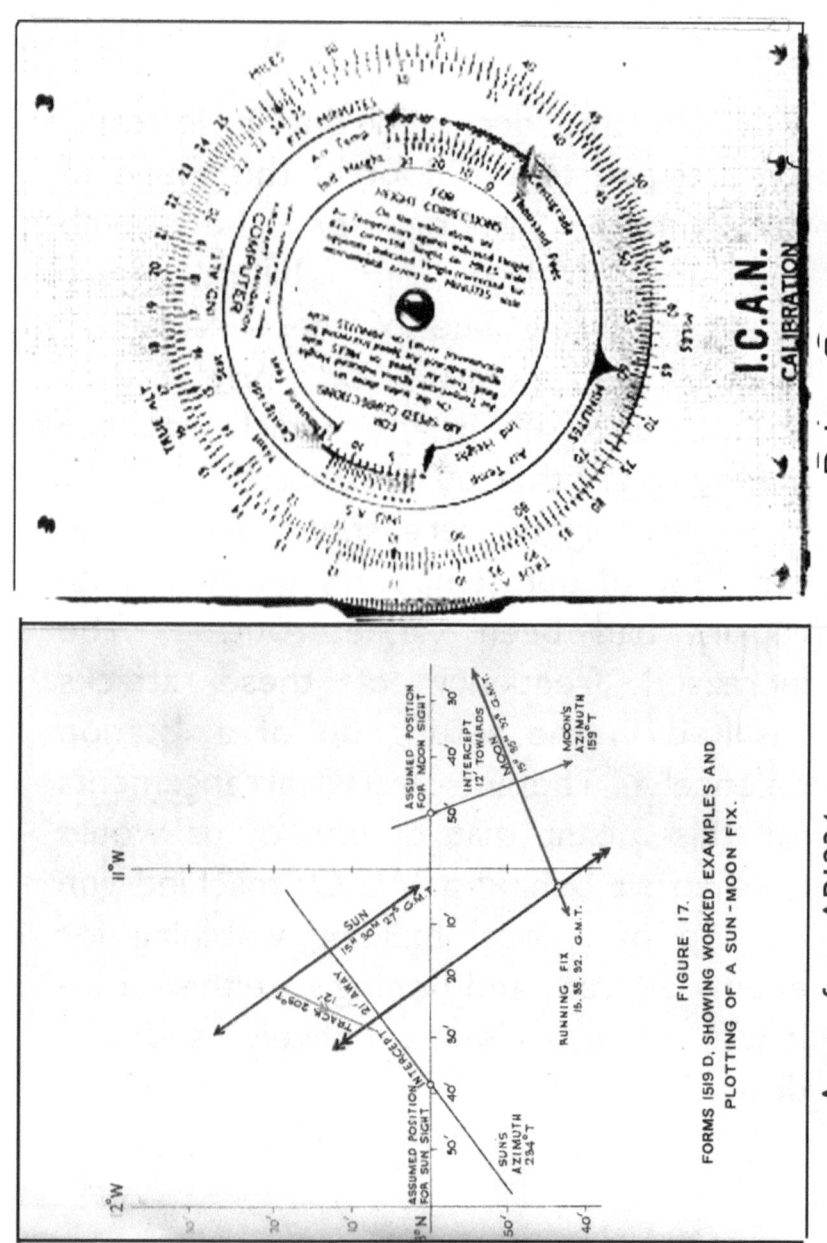

Dalton Computer

FIGURE 17.

FORMS 1519 D, SHOWING WORKED EXAMPLES AND
PLOTTING OF A SUN-MOON FIX.

A page from API234

48

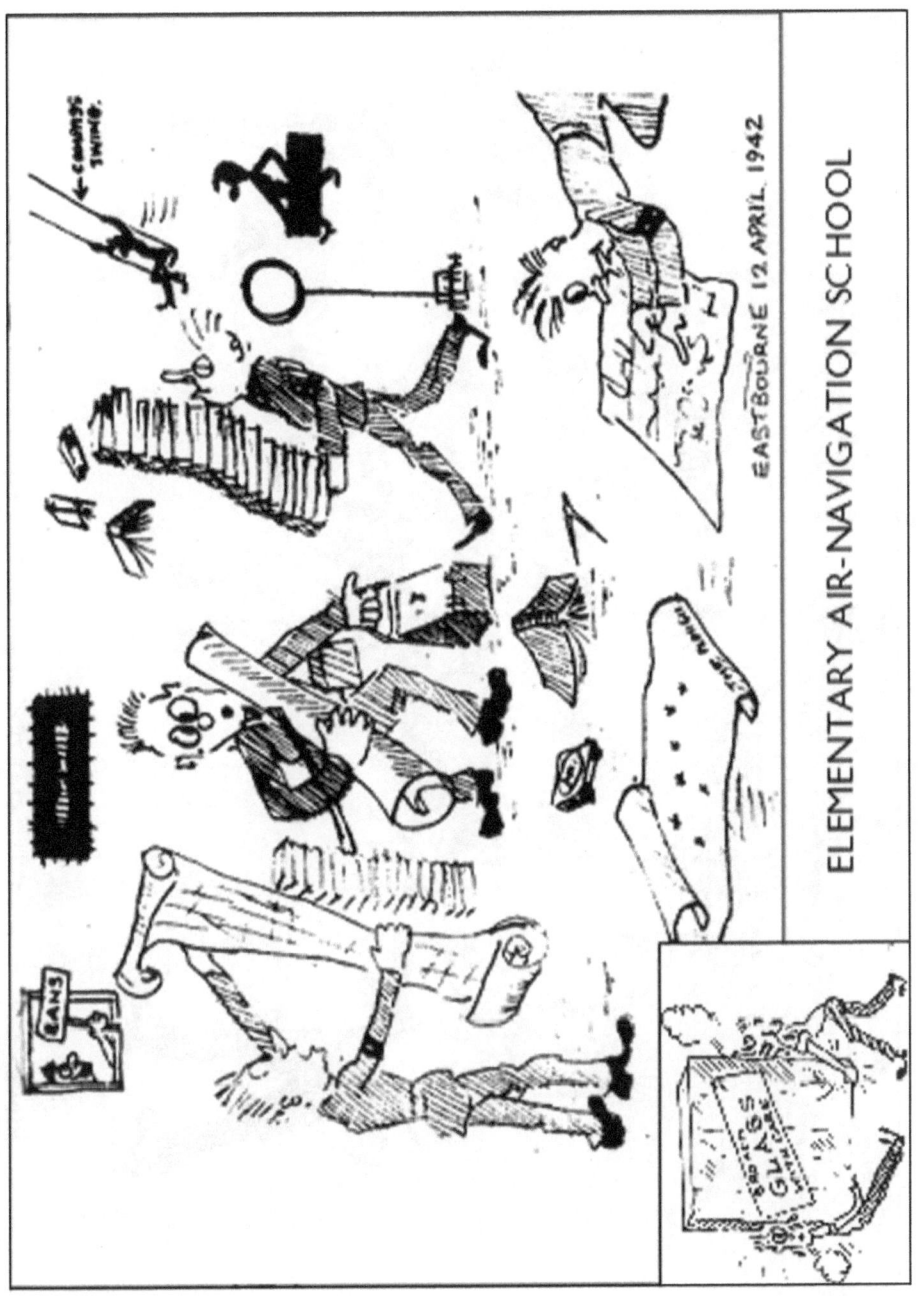

ELEMENTARY AIR-NAVIGATION SCHOOL

"COME ON – PUT SOMETHING INTO IT – AND AGAIN !"

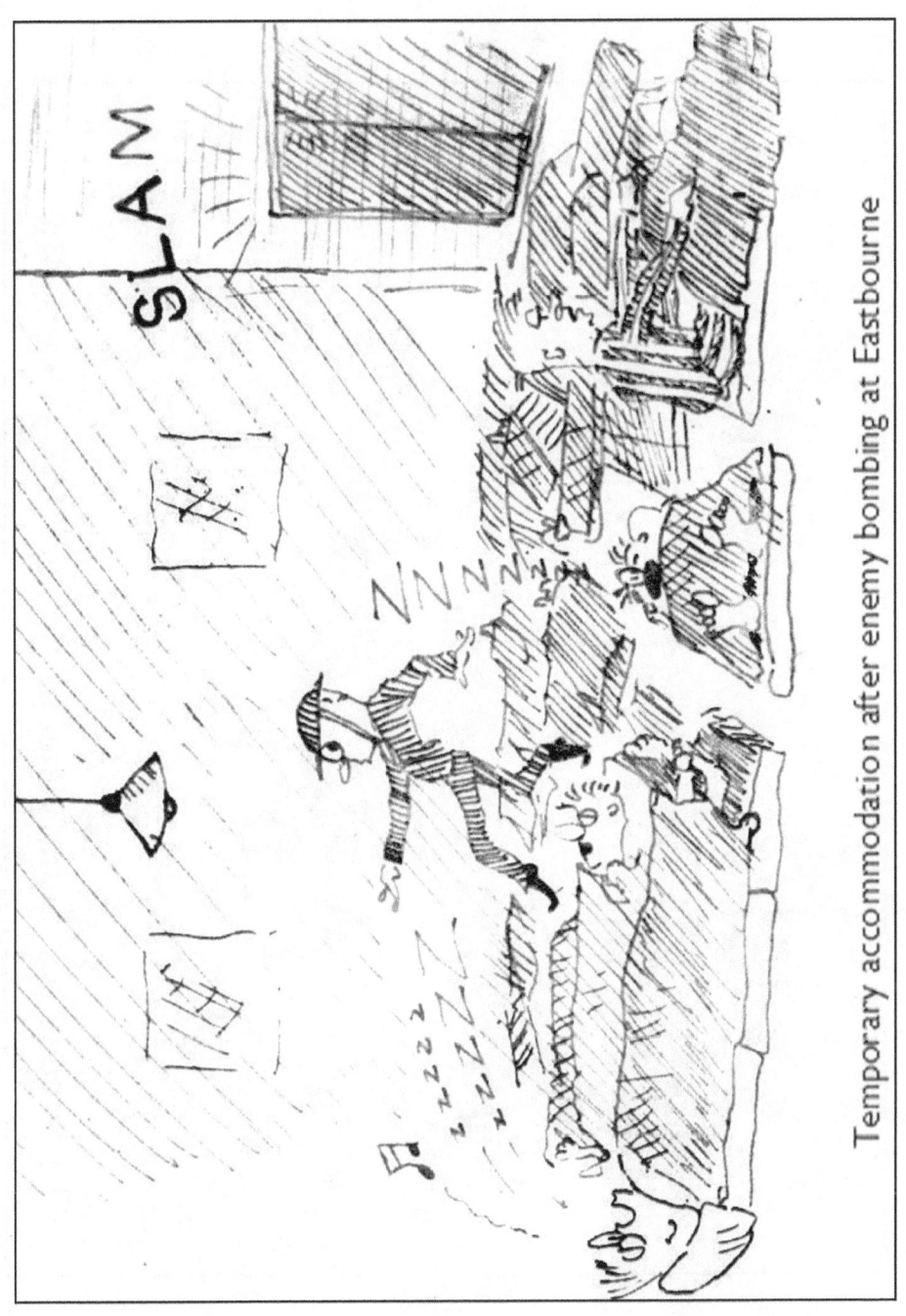

Temporary accommodation after enemy bombing at Eastbourne

There goes our beauty sleep!

During our Aircraft recognition sessions we had come to associate square cut wing tips with the M.E.109E and, on one occasion our intrepid A.A. gunner spotted such an aircraft circling the town apparently looking for a target. There was a burst of V.G.O. gunfire wide of the aircraft, which flew off. Following this, we were summoned by our Flight Commander who showed us, with some urgency, the true identification of the aircraft - the new North American Mustang!

Our astronomy studies often extended into the night with shadowy figures moving along the sea front taking star shots with the R.A.F. Bubble Sextant under clear skies free of light pollution. These activities must have been viewed with great suspicion by the local constabulary!

Meteorology, bomb-aiming theory and dinghy drill were also included in the course. Dinghy drill was practised at the local swimming baths and, to 'inspire confidence', non-swimmers were required to jump from the high diving platform wearing full flying kit including a "Mae West" life jacket!

This was followed by lots of spluttering and scrambling as we climbed into a bobbing rubber dinghy. Needless to say, that by the end of the course, we all learned to swim at least one length of the swimming bath!

In the final summing up at the end of our course the importance was stressed of the use of diagrams when answering examination questions. Following our submissions to the Central Examination Board and a short spell of home leave, we returned to Eastbourne for a period of revision with some drill (including 'dinghy' of course) and more cross country runs to Beachy Head to keep us fit.

The relief and joy of our examination success was somewhat tempered by the news that our next stop was to be A.C.D.W. Brighton once again!!

Regular Medical checks were all important

Gunnery practice with a Vicker's Gas-operated machine gun

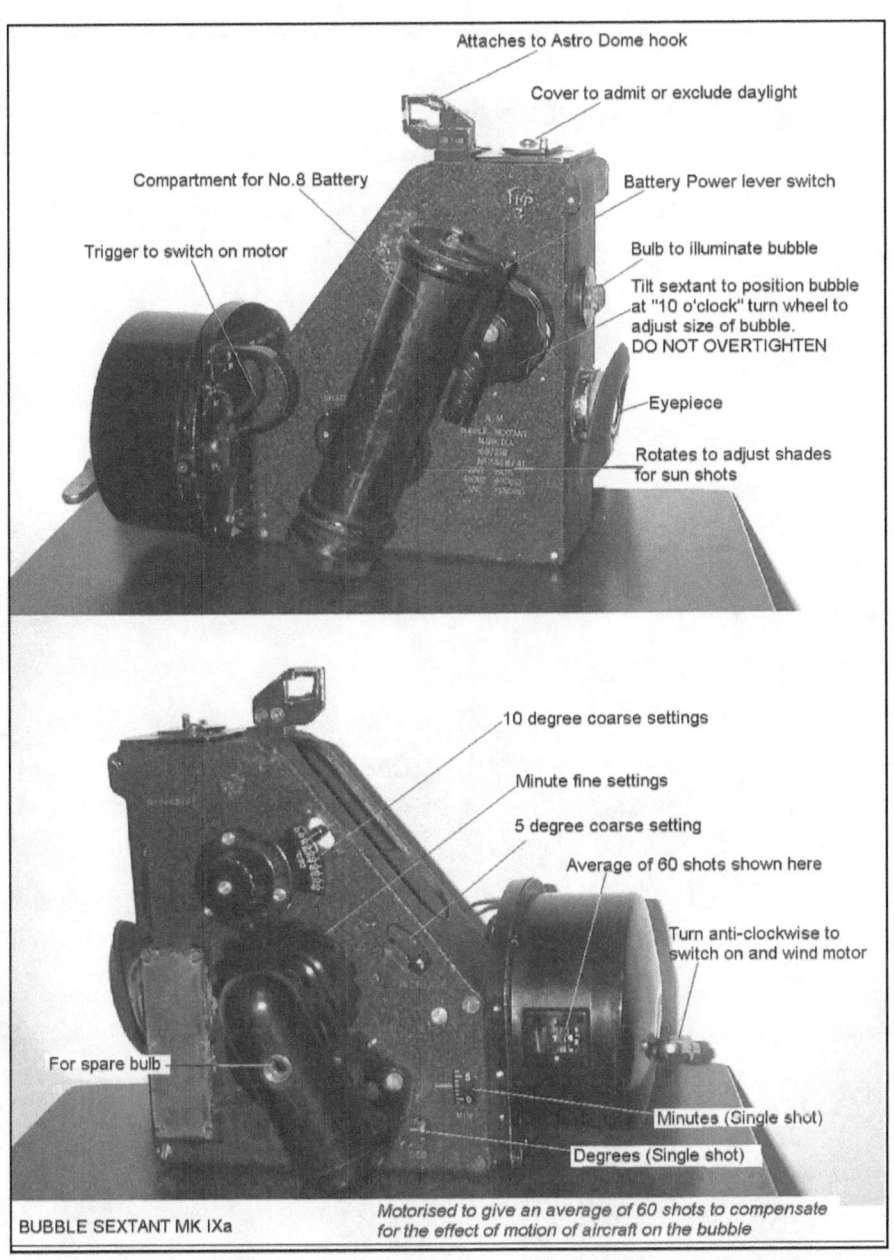

Attaches to Astro Dome hook

Cover to admit or exclude daylight

Compartment for No.8 Battery

Battery Power lever switch

Trigger to switch on motor

Bulb to illuminate bubble

Tilt sextant to position bubble at "10 o'clock" turn wheel to adjust size of bubble.
DO NOT OVERTIGHTEN

Eyepiece

Rotates to adjust shades for sun shots

10 degree coarse settings

Minute fine settings

5 degree coarse setting

Average of 60 shots shown here

Turn anti-clockwise to switch on and wind motor

For spare bulb

Minutes (Single shot)

Degrees (Single shot)

BUBBLE SEXTANT MK IXa

Motorised to give an average of 60 shots to compensate for the effect of motion of aircraft on the bubble

"BUT OFFICER, ALL I SAID WAS 'THERE IS ALPHACCA!'"

RESTING AFTER THE COURSE

6 FLIGHT : D SQDN. No I E.A.N.S. EASTBOURNE JUNE 1942

CHAPTER SEVEN

MOVING ON

BEFORE we made the short move along the coast we all enjoyed a spell of home leave and this time, although we did not realize it, we were on embarkation leave. Brighton had changed little since our previous visit. "Bull" (extreme or exaggerated disciplines) was still the main preoccupation, and it wasn't long before we were cleaning and polishing and arranging our bedding in that all-important perfectly dimensioned cube shaped pack! It was a great relief when, after only seven days, our next move was announced which turned out to be a train journey north to a Personnel Distribution Centre.

When we arrived at P.D.C. West Kirby in Cheshire the camp presented a scene of utter desolation being mainly composed of row upon row of wooden huts. Each hut accommodated about three-dozen men and was furnished with rickety wooden two-tier bunks. The whole area was fenced with barbed wire with open country beyond.

The next seven days were filled with feverish activity including F.F.I. examinations and many inoculations together with "kitting" parades and meal queues. Tropical kit was issued which, one wag suggested, meant that we were going to the North Pole! Much time was spent in packing kit bags marked with a series of rings which were used to aid sorting later on. We were summoned to a meeting by an elderly Air Commodore who informed us that we were going overseas and would be completing our air-navigation training, flying in the clear and sunny climate of South Africa.

On the following day, we boarded the s.s. Volendam at Liverpool, escorted under the watchful eyes of the R.A.F. Police. The vessel was a converted cargo boat; the "conversion" mainly consisting of the installation of wooden mess tables with forms for seating in the hold which was reached by a wooden steps from the deck above. Over the tables there were strategically placed hooks from which to hang hammocks for sleeping at night.

We set sail from Liverpool in a northerly direction, which seemed to cast some doubt as to our promised destination. Our eventual arrival in the Clyde off Greenock and the sight of the many ships assembled there made us realise that we would be part of a convoy. After a few days we headed out into the Atlantic at nine knots in convoy maintaining a steady westerly course.

After many days sailing we eventually turned south and consigned ourselves to the steady routine of life raft drills and inspections combined with the sound of depth charges being dropped by Destroyers circling the outer fringe of the convoy. The loss of salt caused by our perspiring in the heat of our cramped quarters brought on an epidemic of acute diarrhoea and sickness. Weakened "volunteer" mess orderlies found great difficulty in negotiating the steps leading down to the troop deck, and, on occasions, a pan of porridge or stew came to a sticky end whilst the unfortunate mess orderly performed an acrobatic 'base over apex' trying to regain his footing. The shortage of food however, did not seriously concern us at this time!

The slinging of hammocks was also quite a feat and produced many strange and precarious variations. At night, the deck was filled with odd shapes suspended and swinging to and fro with the motion of the ship.   On and on we sailed until, on one mid August afternoon we heard the cry "land ahoy!"   As we slowly approached the West African coast, green hot and steaming under the tropical sun, the air was filled with a smell reminiscent of overcooked spinach as we anchored at Freetown.   "This is the white man's grave!" said our usual "expert", and we were relieved when, after five days, we sailed out of the harbour to resume our journey.

We rounded the Cape of Good Hope to the sound of depth charges dropped by our naval escorts and, after sailing eastwards for a day or so, we eventually turned northwards and, on the 30th August we headed towards land, it was the end of our voyage.   As we drew near to the dockside at Durban we made out the imposing figure of a woman dressed all in white with a powerful voice singing "Land of Hope and Glory!" -- what a memorable and heart warming reception!

It was wonderful to be on dry land once again and, at a camp, under canvas, on the outskirts of Durban, we were able to enjoy a good meal at last. At breakfast we helped ourselves from large open tins labelled with red tomatoes. Should we put this with the bacon? We were soon to discover that it was delicious tomato jam and should be spread on the bread and butter! Kit inspections were made outside our tents following which the usual paper work and medical checks were completed. Our skill at potato peeling was, of course, tested in the open air.

The stay in Durban was quite short and, following an unforgettable glorious long train journey in first class accommodation travelling through the wonderful mountain scenery of the Drakensburgs, we arrived at No.48 Air School, Woodbrook, East London, ready to put our Navigation Theory into practice.

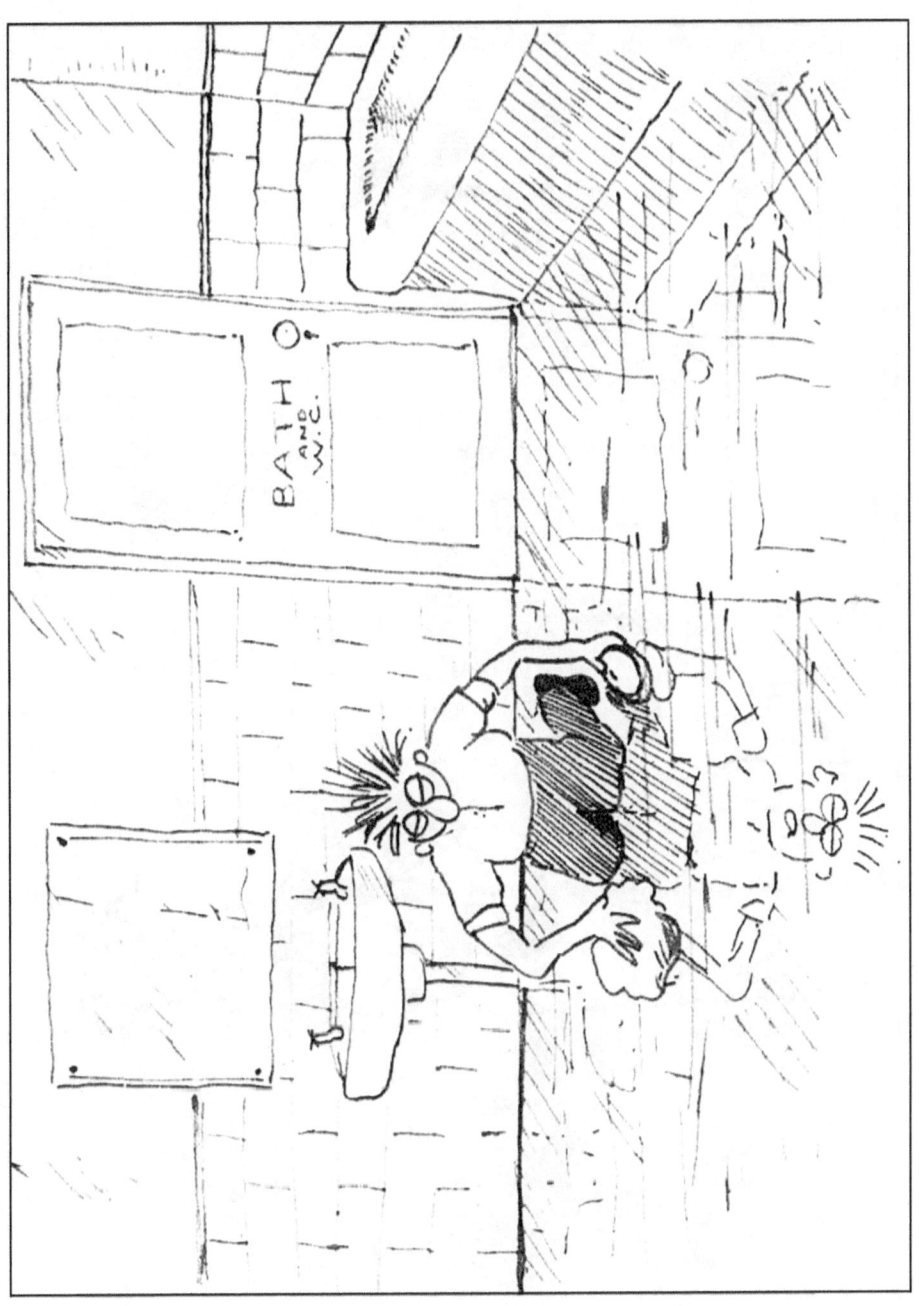

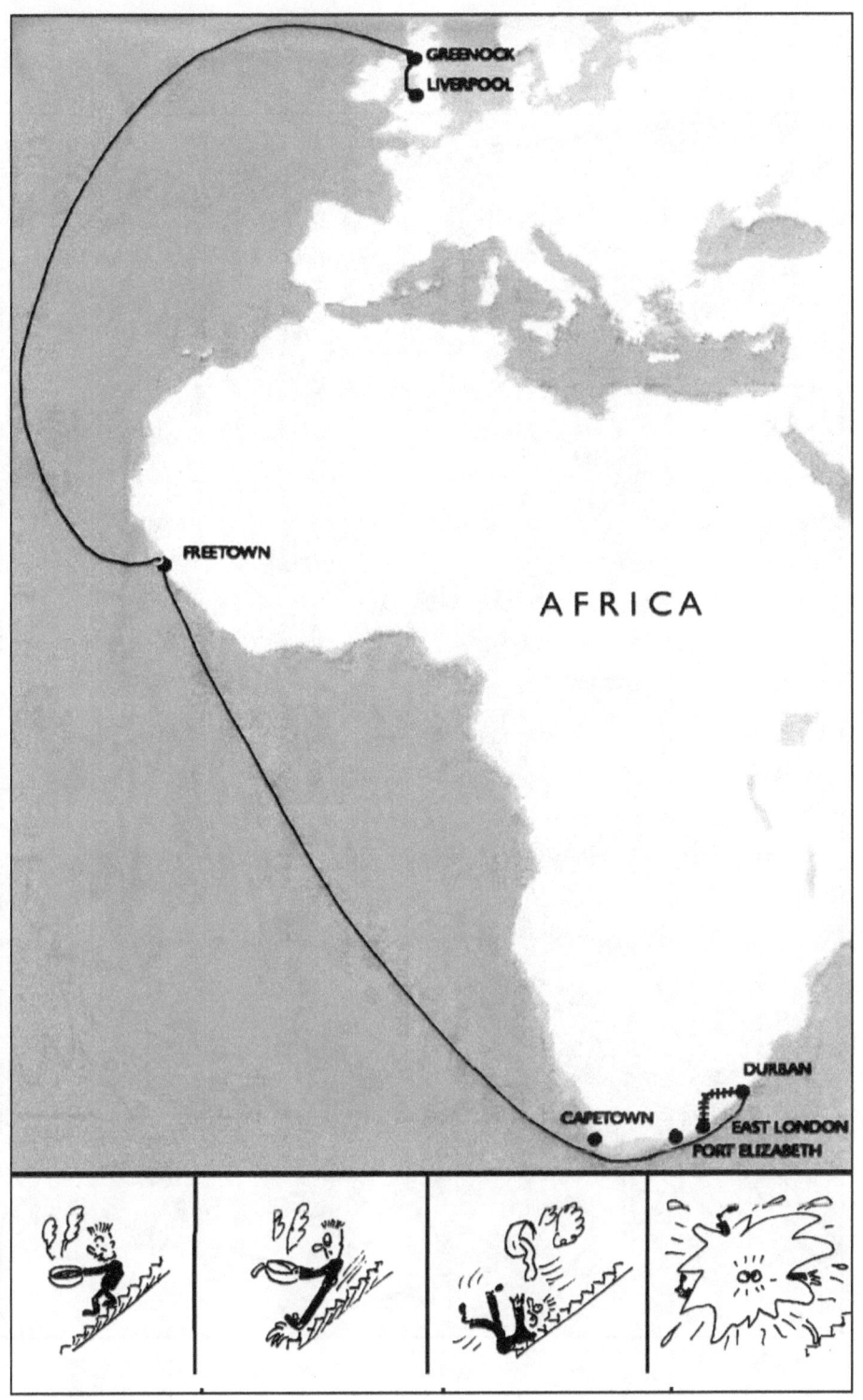

YOU'LL SOON GET THE HANG OF IT!

D
U
R
B
A
N

CHAPTER EIGHT

AIR EXPERIENCE

AT WOODBROOK we began two months of intensive study, polishing up our navigation theory in preparation for our forthcoming excursion into the air. The result of all our training in England was to be put to the test in the twin-engined Avro Anson aircraft which was well suited for the purpose due to the fact that the upper part of the fuselage was covered in perspex windows. In the clear South African atmosphere we could often see our destination soon after being airborne!

Within four days of our arrival we found ourselves in the air, on a two hour flight entitled "Air experience". For some it proved to be an "experience" never to be forgotten! Air sickness appeared to be quite common when trainees went into the air for the first time, and it was carefully monitored during subsequent trips to ensure that it was only caused by temporary nervousness and could be overcome. If the problem persisted the unfortunate airman was failed.

One of the navigator's duties in the Anson was the winding up and down of the undercarriage. This was performed by cranking a handle situated alongside the pilot and, the physical effort during hot weather combined with the smell of dope, which was used to treat the fabric covering of the aircraft, was often the final straw in encouraging our stomach to part company with its contents!

Off duty moments were the signal for a mass exodus of all trainees into East London where we encountered the great generosity and friendliness of the local residents. They made us most welcome and groups were regularly invited into their homes to partake of dinner and tea. There were many tearful farewells when the time came for our final departure.

In all we completed about eighty hours in the air putting all our air navigation theory into practice as well as doing photographic and bomb-aiming exercises. All this practical work was assessed together with examination papers covering the theory. Time was also spent on the parade ground being drilled by a South African Sergeant Major. This included rifle drill in preparation for the end of course passing out parade when our names would be called in turn for presentation of our Observer's brevet (O), later to be replaced in England by the new Navigator's brevet (N) when the introduction of larger bomber crews made necessary the separate duty of Bomb Aimer, who wore a 'B' brevet.

Following the celebration of our success, together with the promotion to the rank of sergeant, we were moved on by train to Cape Town.   At a transit camp within sight of Table Mountain we were given sacks and a supply of straw to make palliasses for our bedding whilst we awaited a ship to take us back home.

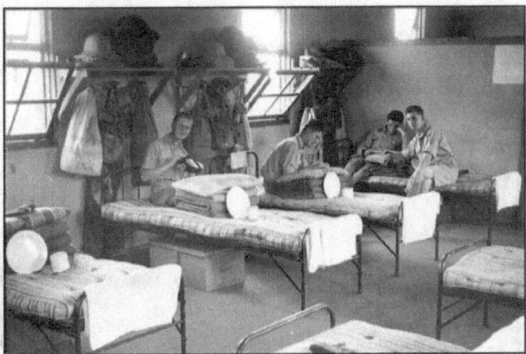

**41 AIR SCHOOL, EAST LONDON
SOUTH AFRICA**

S.A.A.F. Form 639
S.A.L.M. Vorm 639

S.A. AIR FORCE.
S.A. LUGMAG.

EXERCISE BOOK
OEFENBOEK

FOR USE IN
VIR GEBRUIK BY

AIR FORCE TRAINING SCHOOLS.
LUGMAGSKOLE.

No....**4.1**....AIR SCHOOL

AIR NAVIGATORS COURSE No. **7**

FROM....**23/11/42**....TO....**26/3/43**

PASS OR FAIL....*Pass*

REMARKS.................................

....

....

M Bank S/.
OFFICER COMMANDING

DATE....**26/3/43**....No....**41**....AIR SCHOOL

PRACTICE IN FLAME FLOAT DROPPING CARRIED OUT

ON THIS COURSE   *M Ollott* F/O I/c COURSE.

Observer Brevet

Navigator Brevet

Where do we go from here?

Macaroni again? Well I'll be bound!

CHAPTER NINE

HOME AGAIN

OUR JOURNEY home on board one of the Castle Line passenger liners was undertaken at speed by a relatively direct route and in the knowledge that we were perhaps moving too fast to be caught by U boats! This time our main occupation during the voyage was performing guard duties over a crowd of Italian prisoners-of-war who were held below decks in similar conditions to those that we 'enjoyed' on our outward journey. Our impression was that they were most happy to be sailing miles away from their campaign in the North African desert and showed no interest whatsoever in escape! Following an uneventful journey we found ourselves back in dear old war torn Blighty for a long awaited home leave and completion of our training.

We then experienced a series of postings to keep us in trim prior to O.T.U. A short spell of map reading from the second open cockpit of a Tiger Moth flying over the Lake District proved to be extremely instructive.

On one occasion, when the pilot must have been feeling bored, he livened up the exercise by looping the aircraft! We spent a month practicing D.R.(Dead Reckoning) Navigation and air photography flying around the Cumberland area and over the Isle of Man in the familiar Avro Anson, although much time was wasted due to bad weather. Our next posting, however, was to be the most important one so far, our new destination being No.10 O.T.U. (Operational Training Unit) at Abingdon in Berkshire.

Stanton Harcourt, a satellite of Abingdon, was to be our new home, and we arrived there on 31st August 1943. Apart from a few Ansons, the main training aircraft here was the Armstrong Whitworth Whitley twin engined bomber affectionately known as the "flying coffin", thankfully due to its long box-like shape rather than its reputation! It was here that at last I found myself teamed up with other airmen to form a bomber crew.

Our ability to operate and fly together as an efficient team was carefully monitored and assessed during the next three-months of our training.

LEVEL THE INSTRUMENT
"The Bombsight must be carefully levelled"

The Metman who used too much hydrogen!

TIGER MOTH

WHITLEY

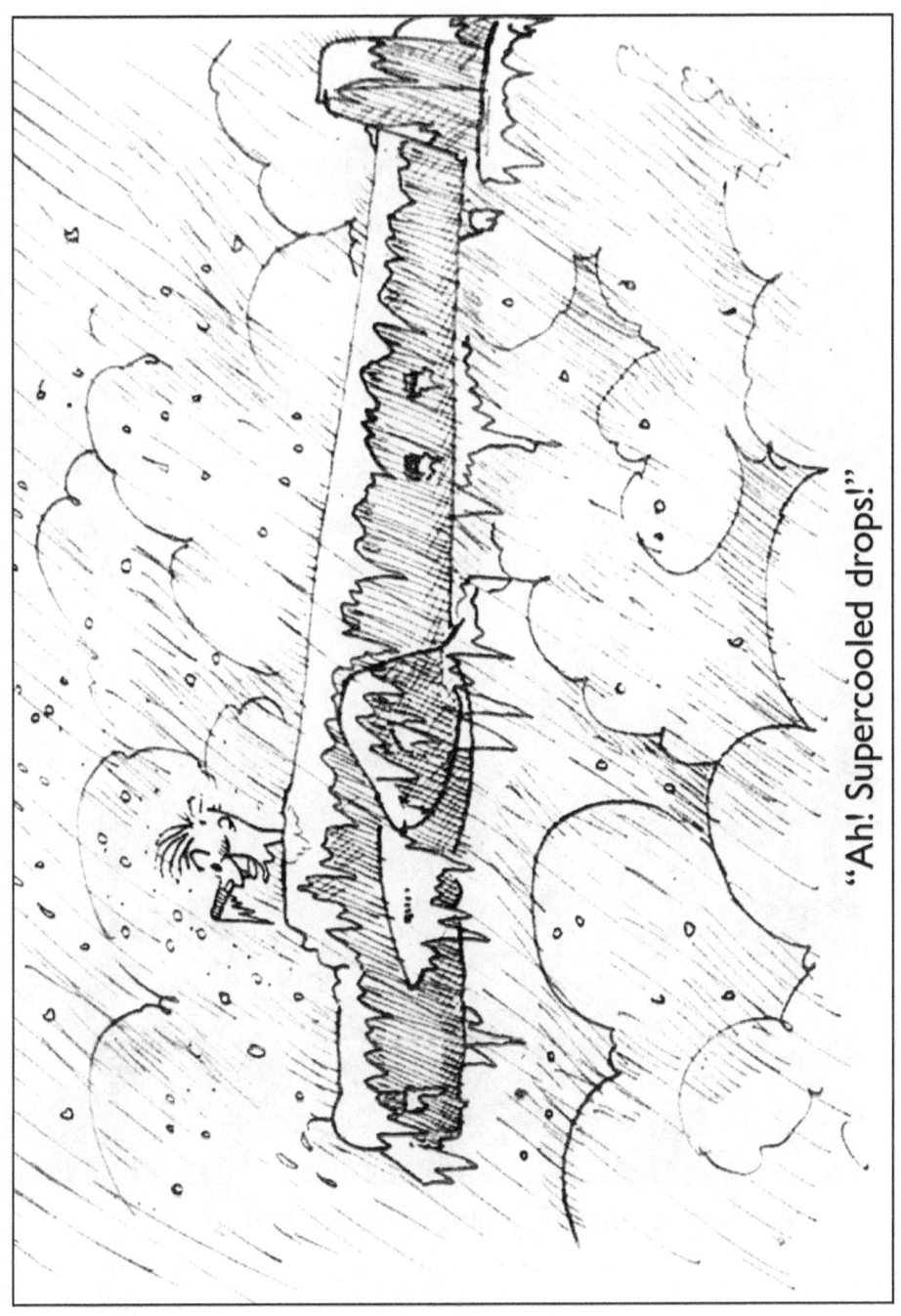

"Ah! Supercooled drops!"

At Operational Training Unit Abingdon 1943

CHAPTER TEN

OPERATIONAL TRAINING

DAY AFTER DAY of circuits and landings (nicknamed "bumps") were carried out as we all familiarised ourselves with the aircraft and equipment. The navigator's collapsible table really lived up to its name, being able to collapse at most inappropriate moments! Cross-country flights and bombing exercises, sometimes carrying a war load, were a regular part of the training programme. Fighter affiliation sorties were sometimes included to give the pilot practice in putting the aircraft into a "corkscrew" routine. This manoeuvre had a similar effect on the internal digestive organs of the aircrew!

At O.T.U., with great security inside a locked building, we were introduced to Radar (Radio Detection and Ranging) which was displayed in the form of matchstick shaped "blips" moving along lines on a green glowing cathode tube. These "blips" were in fact able to indicate an aircraft's distance from aerials situated around the English coastline and then could be read off against a calibrated scale and plotted on a specially printed chart. The system was code-named "Gee" and was used extensively as a navigational aid during raids until eventually suffering from jamming by the enemy.

On the 19th November 1943 our flight briefing was of a more serious nature and gave us details of our first operation over enemy occupied territory. The target was Versailles near Paris and our task was to carry a bundles of leaflets for distribution from the air.

O.T.U., operations were usually timed to coincide with the main force of Bomber Command aircraft heading further east and carrying a more lethal load in their bomb bays. The whole was intended to confuse enemy radar and hopefully saturate the enemy defence system.

Anti-aircraft gunners and fighter aircraft showed disapproval of our presence and attacked us from the ground and in the air. We were relieved when we had dropped our leaflets and had finally left the continent behind us. An air raid over the south coast of England resulted in our being diverted to

Exeter where we landed safely after four and quarter hours. It was reassuring for me to know that my navigation had survived whilst working under pressure. A few days later we flew our aircraft back to Stanton Harcourt and, following one more air test, our course at Operational Training Unit was finished.

Our conversion to four engined heavy bombers began on 18th December when we reported to No.1663 Heavy Conversion Unit, Rufforth, situated about three miles to the west of York. We were now to fly as a crew in the very impressive Handley Page Halifax bomber, and soon began the familiar routine of circuits and bumps, cross-country flights, practice bombing and fighter affiliation.

By the time we had completed our term at Rufforth, we all felt great confidence in our ability to function as a great little team, having successfully completed all tasks allotted to us with most in really trying winter conditions.

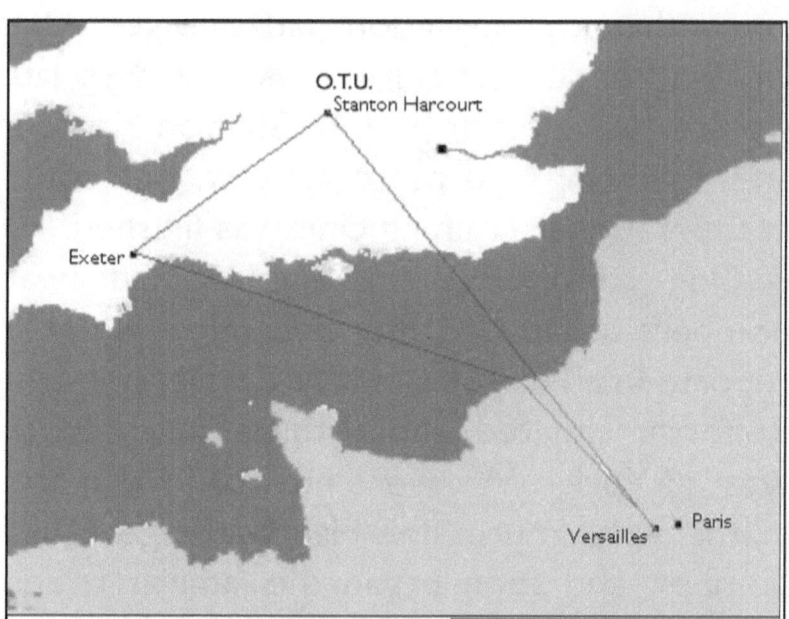

O.T.U.
Stanton Harcourt

Exeter

Versailles • Paris

Front and reverse of leaflet dropped over Versailles

Les Allemands perdent la Bataille du Dnieper

LA SITUATION ÉVOLUE RAPIDE-MENT DANS TOUT LE SECTEUR DU DNIEPER INFÉRIEUR, OÙ LE SORT DU GROUPE D'ARMÉES MANNSTEIN EST EN JEU.

Kiev subit une pression croissante. Après l'occupa-tion de Mélitopol, qui fut précédée par des combats de rue d'une extrême violence, Dnepropetrovsk est tom-bée aux mains des Russes à la suite d'un nouveau passage du Dnieper.

Dans la steppe de Nogaïsk, à l'ouest de Mélitopol, les Russes ont rompu le front allemand sur une largeur de 100 kms., et refoulent un ennemi désemparé vers l'isthme de Perekop et l'es-tuaire du Dnieper. Le saillant russe basé sur le Dnieper entre Krementchoug et Dnepropetrovsk s'allonge rapidement vers Nikolaïev, à l'embouchure du Boug. Dans cette direction l'Armée rouge a atteint les fau-bourgs de Krivoï Rog, à mi-chemin entre le Dnieper et la Mer Noire. Il semble que de forts contin-gents ennemis aient été encerclés, et les *Junkers* 52 de transport qui ravitaillèrent la VIe Armée de Paulus à Stalingrad) ont fait leur apparition.

L'Agence d'information alle-mande de Scandinavie annonce que les Russes jettent dans la bataille du saillant d'énormes masses de blindés et d'artillerie, suivies par de nombreuses divi-sions d'infanterie. En outre, l'Aviation rouge attaque sans répit les embarcadères ferro-viaires, de moins en moins nom-breux, par lesquels l'ennemi doit évacuer ses troupes à bref délai s'il veut éviter le désastre.

Les Allemands contre-atta-quent férocement. mais locale-ment, sur les flancs et la pointe du grand saillant russe, sans grand effet d'ailleurs et avec des pertes terribles.

Le moment approche rapide-ment où le Haut - Com-mandement allemand devra, ou bien déclencher une contre-offen-sive d'envergure pour tenter de rétablir une situation exception-nellement grave, ou bien ordonner une retraite générale qui aurait toutes les chances de se transformer en déroute. Le rédacteur militaire du *Times* déclare, après une étude

(Suite à la page 2)

Forces navales légères en action

LES unités légères de la *Royal Navy* ont démontré une fois de plus leur vigilance en mer du Nord, au cours d'un récent engagement qui les mit aux prises avec des vedettes lance-torpilles allemandes.

Une trentaine de ces vedettes rapides tentèrent de s'approcher d'un convoi allié qui filait le long de la côte est de l'Angleterre. En une série de combats qui durèrent 5 heures, quatre vedettes allemandes furent coulées, et sept endommagées, tandis que l'escorte britannique de destroyers et de canonnières rapides. Le convoi et les navires de guerre britan-niques ne subirent aucune perte.

Un groupe de cinq vedettes allemandes fut d'abord intercepté par le destroyer *Pytchley* qui les contraignit à abandonner le combat après avoir réussi des coups au but sur l'une d'elles.

Plus tard, les canonnières anglaises entrèrent en action contre une nouvelle flotille alle-mande, infligeant de sérieux dégâts à l'un des navires ennemis. Cependant, le destroyer *Wor-cester* engageait le combat au canon avec un autre groupe ennemi, faisant sauter une vedette et en endommageant une autre. Une quatrième flotille alle-mande fut ensuite interceptée par une flotille britannique. Dans le bref combat qui s'ensuivit, deux navires allemands sautèrent et un troisième fut éperonné et coulé par une canonnière britannique.

REVEIL EN SURSAUT

"La certitude somnam-buliste avec laquelle le Fuehrer envisage l'avenir et fait ses plans, anticipant leur achève-ment, nous assure qu'au-jourd'hui il conservera l'ini-tiative et que lui seul dictera le cours de la guerre."

Voelkischer Beobachter.
11.11.41

Le chef de l'escadrille Normandie donne ses instructions.

En Italie avances alliées dans des conditions difficiles

La VIIIe Armée a tra-versé le Trigno — un fleuve qui prend sa source dans les Apennins et se jette dans l'Adriatique — et a établi une tête de pont sur la rive nord.

L'ennemi retranché derrière une solide ligne de résistance, n'abandonna le terrain qu'après de durs combats et lança des contre-attaques qui furent toutes repoussées.

Avant de se retirer les Alle-mands firent sauter tous les ponts derrière eux. Dès le début de l'attaque, les troupes du général Montgomery prirent Mon-tenero puis délogèrent l'ennemi de plusieurs positions élevées qu'il occupait. Deux autres villes sont tombées depuis aux mains des Alliés dans ce secteur : Lucita et Campochiano.

Le passage du Trigno est, comme le passage du Volturne effectué huit jours auparavant par la Ve Armée, une opération amphibie de petite envergure dont

(Suite à la page 2)

la réussite n'est pas accompagnée de gains en terrain considérables. De l'autre côté du Trigno il y a des montagnes. Sur la rive nord du Volturne, la plaine côtière est sillonnée de canaux, de fossés de drainage et de cours d'eau na-turels qui ralentissent le mouve-ment des opérations. La Ve Armée ne peut utiliser qu'une seule route dans cette plaine, celle qui passe par Capoue et mène à Formia.

Après s'être retiré dans les montagnes autour de Mandragone et Venafro, brûlant et détruisant tout sur son passage, l'ennemi a déclenché une violente contre-attaque dans la région d'Alife, dans la vallée au nord-ouest du Volturne. Les Allemands qui avaient engagé dans la bataille de l'artillerie et des chars pour appuyer l'infanterie, ont dû battre en retraite, laissant sur le terrain un bon nombre de chars.

Tout cela montre que les opéra-tions d'Italie sont lentes et coûteuses et qu'une armée qui a sauté la Méditerranée pour venir

(Suite à la page 2)

En Méditerranée : Un convoi allié a été attaqué récemment au large de la côte nord-africaine par l'ennemi avec des Dorniers, armés de bombes-planeurs radio-dirigées et avec des Heinkels munis de torpilles. Des pilotes français sur Airacobra armés de canons et de mitrailleuses, disper-sèrent les attaquants en abattant trois et endom-mageant sérieusement quatre autres appareils.

En Russie : Le groupe de chasse Normandie qui co-opère avec l'Aviation russe a été cité par le général Giraud à l'Ordre de l'Armée aérienne française. Voici le texte de la citation :

"Au cours d'opérations offensives menées dans la région d'Yelnia, du 18 août au 4 septembre, 1943, avec la participation de 13, puis de 14, puis de 12 pilotes, le groupe Normandie, en quinze jours de combats très durs, accomplit une tâche remarquable en abat-tant 20 avions ennemis homologues, probablement deux autres et en endom-mageant 10, tout en con-servant un moral remar-quable, malgré la perte d'un pilote tué et de 3 pilotes disparus. Cette citation comporte l'attribution de la Croix de Guerre avec palme."

Dans une déclaration re-produite par Combat, M. Bogomoloff, Ambassadeur de l'U.R.S.S. à Alger, dit : "J'ai eu l'occasion de voir vos jeunes aviateurs du groupe Normandie qui mènent un magnifique et fraternel combat dans l'Armée rouge. Un pays qui possède une telle jeu-nesse mérite sa place à la victoire commune avec les autres puissances alliées."

F.155

Four page leaflet dropped over Versailles

Le général Smuts donne un aperçu stratégique

Le 19 octobre, au Guild-hall de Londres où il était reçu par le Lord-Maire, le général Smuts, au cours d'un discours sur les progrès de la guerre et les problèmes de la paix, a déclaré que l'assaut final serait lancé sur la forteresse hitlérienne "aussitôt que possible l'année prochaine."

Voici les passages principaux de son discours. Après avoir dépeint le changement intervenu dans la fortune des Alliés depuis l'été 1942, où l'ennemi était à Stalingrad et aux portes de l'Egypte, le général Smuts a dit :

"Ce grand changement ne fait que renforcer ma certitude que, à mesure que nous nous éloignerons de la phase défensive, les événements prendront un tour de plus en plus catastrophique pour l'ennemi ; crises et paroxysmes seront de plus en plus vifs et soudains, jusqu'à son écroulement définitif.

"Le rétablissement de nos communications vitales, la con-

Suite de la page 1

La Crimée est menacée

approfondie de la propagande ennemie de ces derniers jours, qu'une telle contre-offensive est improbable : les Allemands ne sont pas assez forts pour l'entreprendre.

Les chemins de fer encore aux mains de l'ennemi dans la boucle du Dnieper sont d'un débit insuffisant pour assurer la retraite de plus d'une fraction du groupe d'armées du sud. Dans un Ordre du Jour annonçant la prise de Dnepropetrovsk, Staline ne parle pas de prisonniers, mais fait état du butin énorme ramassé par les Russes. Il semblerait donc que les troupes allemandes défendant ce secteur du Dnieper ont été en grande partie évacuées, *mais sans leur matériel lourd.*

A moins d'un renversement dramatique de la situation, *ce* genre d'évacuation servira peut-être avant peu de modèle pour la plus grande partie des armées allemandes en Russie méridionale.

Autre preuve de la retraite allemande prend des proportions catastrophiques : sur le chemin de Krivol Rog, les Allemands ont laissé des villages intacts, avec leurs greniers pleins du grain de la récolte, et sans déporter la population ou procéder à leurs habituelles "représailles."

Plus au sud, un porte-parole militaire allemand, l'évacuation de la Crimée est en cours. La Crimée est un objectif de la plus haute importance stratégique que les Russes ont une bonne chance de cueillir au passage, presque sans coup férir.

quête de bases essentielles pour l'attaque contre la Forteresse hitlérienne, la capitulation d'une grande puissance européenne, le ralliement de la Flotte italienne, — tout ceci doit être mis à l'actif de notre stratégie méditerranéenne.

". . . Nous pouvons compter sur d'autres avances encore, surtout dans le sud et le sud-est de l'Europe. Lorsque viendra l'hiver, nous aurons investi de près Hitler au centre de sa forteresse, et nos préparatifs seront en cours pour le grand assaut de toutes les armes qui aura lieu l'année prochaine."

Secours international

"Il sera vite pensé au relèvement économique de l'univers tant que cette impérieuse mission humanitaire n'aura pas été menée à bien. Quelque place être notre politique de réparations après cette guerre, du moins commencera-t-elle par le travail essentiel de secours international, dont dépendra le retour de l'univers à de meilleures conditions de vie : démolir pour gagner le temps.

Dans ces conditions, la prise de Rome ne sera pas aisée. En effet, comme l'a dit le général Alexander, "tous les chemins mènent à Rome, mais la route de Rome est

Le rôle des E.U.

"Dans cet assaut contre l'Europe d'Hitler, les Etats-Unis joueront sans nul doute un rôle de premier plan — peut-être le premier rôle. Malgré leur apport déjà grand, leur rôle dans la guerre jusqu'ici a été celui que qui, dès le début, avait été prévu : celui d'arsenal de la démocratie. Leur effort industriel, déjà prodigieux, monte toujours vers des cimes inimaginables. Mais jusqu'ici, les ressources en hommes des Etats-Unis ont été justement considérés comme notre grande réserve stratégique à l'ouest, à utiliser dans les ultimes opérations de la guerre.

"Alors que chacun des Alliés fera tout son possible pour provoquer la décision, les Etats-Unis, partenaire nouveau venu, mais le plus frais et le plus puissant de tous, auront peut-être le rôle décisif à jouer dans ce dernier acte du drame.

Le temps presse

Puis, le général Smuts, parlant du facteur temps, a montré à quel point la situation tragique de l'Europe préoccupait les Alliés.

"Le temps presse", a-t-il dit. "Dans cette cinquième année de guerre, le facteur temps prime tout : dorénavant, chaque jour compte. Déjà les circonstances morales et physiques des pays occupés sont indescriptibles. Si nous voulons épargner à l'Europe un immense désastre, nous devons tenir pour souveraine la nécessité de terminer la guerre dans le plus bref délai possible. Pour soutenir la guerre, Hitler vide toute l'Europe occupée de ses vivres, de ses richesses et de sa main-d'œuvre. Partout, avec une cruauté sans précédent, les populations sous la botte sont réduites à la misère et au désespoir. Les souffrances morales et physiques des peuples opprimés dépassent tout ce que l'homme a connu dans les temps les plus barbares. Les ténèbres d'une monstruosité, que n'éclaire plus la charité chrétienne, couvrent la face de l'Europe nazie en ce vingtième siècle. Ces ténèbres, il faudra les dissiper avant peu si l'Europe doit être sauvée."

Passant ensuite aux tâches de paix et de reconstruction qui attendront les Alliés après la libération, le général Smuts a poursuivi :

"On a dit très justement que la paix fera partie intégrante de la guerre, qu'il aura été vain de gagner la guerre et la paix n'est pas, elle aussi, gagnée. Mais la tâche de relever l'Europe des ruines de la guerre sera plus urgente encore. La simple né-

cessité de nourrir, abriter et soigner les populations de détresse taxera nos ressources autant que la guerre elle-même. Et il faudra également atténuer les conséquences psychologiques de cette situation pour empêcher que l'Europe ne sombre dans l'anarchie et la barbarie. L'intérêt public non moins que nos sentiments personnels exigeront que nous nous attaquions résolument à cette tâche grave entre toutes.

LE NORMANDIE EST RENFLOUE

Le *Normandie* est maintenant complètement renfloué ; il a été dirigé vers les chantiers de la Marine des Etats-Unis. Il va être aménagé en transporteur de troupes ; ce travail demandera neuf mois au minimum.

Rebaptisé le *Lafayette*, il entrera en service dans la flotte à la disposition des Nations Unies pour amener à pied d'œuvre les troupes alliées.

La route de Rome est minée

(SUITE DE LA PAGE I)

attaquer l'ennemi sur son terrain en Europe, ne peut pas franchir en quelques jours des montagnes bien défendues. L'avance est régulière, mais elle se fait kilomètre par kilomètre, L'ennemi recule sans cesse avec une seule idée en tête : démolir pour gagner du temps.

Dans ces conditions, la prise de Rome ne sera pas aisée. En effet, comme l'a dit le général Alexander, "tous les chemins mènent à Rome, mais la route de Rome est

Tous les renseignements concordent pour indiquer que les Allemands ont envoyé en Italie des renforts importants prélevés sur leur réserve stratégique. Ceci explique pourquoi Mannstein n'a pas pu jeter dans la bataille du Dnieper des divisions fraîches en quantités suffisantes pour contenir les attaques furieuses de l'Armée rouge.

Le général Alexander a déclaré à ce sujet :—

"Quand nous avons débarqué, dit-il, "il n'y avait que

quatre ou cinq divisions allemandes en Italie. Il y a maintenant probablement 35 à 40 divisions en Italie et dans les Balkans.

"Il serait inexact de dire que les Allemands ont retiré des divisions du front de l'Est pour les envoyer combattre en Italie. La vérité c'est qu'ils ont été contraints de vider leurs réserves de divisions qui auraient pu être utilisées sur le front russe.

Si, sur terre, les Allemands peuvent, tout en perdant du terrain, gagner un peu de temps, dans les airs la situation est différente. Sur toute la largeur du front des Ve et VIIIe Armées, les aviations alliées bombardent sans cesse des positions ennemies situées de seize à quarante kilomètres en arrière des premières lignes. Les attaques aériennes continuent contre les moyens de transport allemands et trois ponts de chemin de fer ont reçu des coups au but : à Albina, près de la côte au nord-ouest de Rome ; à Montalto di Castro, au nord-ouest de Rome également, et à Masciano, entre Perugio et Terni.

Les communications allemandes en Italie sont soumises à un pilonnage incessant. L'attaque contre la gare de Bolzano.

LES BOMBARDEMENTS SUR L'ALLEMAGNE

Au profit de la Résistance française

Le Commissariat à l'Information du C.F.L.N. a publié le communiqué suivant :

"Un décret du Comité Français de la Libération Nationale organise officiellement la souscription nationale pour la Résistance française. Cette souscription, ouverte sur l'initiative de la France Combattante, est placée sous le patronage d'un Comité d'honneur, présidé par le général Catroux, Gouverneur-Général de l'Algérie.

"L'organisation de la souscription est confiée à un Comité exécutif central, placé sous la présidence du professeur Capitant."

Les sommes réunies seront affectées à la fourniture de vivres, de vêtements et d'armes aux patriotes français.

Arrestation du général Bergeret

Sur ordre du C.F.L.N., le général Jean Bergeret, ancien ministre de l'Air de Vichy, a été arrêté.

Selon la radio d'Alger, il est inculpé d'avoir incité les Français à combattre les Britanniques en Syrie, d'avoir donné des armes aux rebelles en Irak, d'avoir permis aux Allemands de se servir de bases aériennes vitales en Syrie en contravention directe des termes de l'armistice.

Coopération navale

L'amiral Cunningham, Chef du Grand E.M. naval britannique, a adressé à l'amiral Lemonnier le message suivant :

"Autrefois, le 21 octobre évoquait les rivalités passées entre nos pays, mais aujourd'hui, nous ne nous souvenons que des grandes traditions navales qui sont communes à nos deux peuples et qui nous animent dans la guerre que nous menons ensemble contre l'ennemi commun."

Sous les nuages de fumée se trouvent les décombres des usines Focke Wulf à Marienbourg, bombardées par les Américains.

Cassel reçoit 1.500 tonnes

CASSEL, CENTRE D'ARMEMENT IMPORTANT SITUÉ À L'EST DE LA RUHR, A ÉTÉ ATTAQUÉE VIOLEMMENT PAR LA R.A.F. DANS LA NUIT DU 22 OCTOBRE.

Des formations très puissantes de gros bombardiers ont jeté plus de 1.500 tonnes de bombes explosives et incendiaires; à la fin de cette attaque concentrée, de larges incendies s'étaient déclarés dans les quartiers industriels.

Tout le long de leur route, les appareils britanniques ont affronté le mauvais temps et des orages. Mais ils trouvèrent une éclaircie au-dessus de l'objectif, ce qui leur permit d'exécuter leur mission.

Les bombardiers les derniers arrivés sur Cassel furent confrontés par des chasseurs de nuit et ils leur livrèrent bataille.

La R.A.F. perdit 44 bombardiers mais la défense allemande fut lourdement éprouvée.

Simultanément, Francfort était bombardée tandis que des bombardiers rapides *Mosquito* s'attaquaient à des objectifs dans la région de Cologne.

Dans l'après-midi du 23 octobre, des bombardiers *Typhoon* ont attaqué des navires allemands mouillés dans la rade de St. Malo. Des coups furent enregistrés sur trois contre-torpilleurs et un bateau-citerne a fait explosion.

Pendant la même période, les aviations anglo-américaines ont pilonné des aérodromes ennemis situés dans le nord de la France et en Hollande.

Après Marienbourg

Les photographies aériennes prises après l'attaque américaine du 9 octobre contre les usines Focke Wulf à Marienbourg, en Prusse orientale, ont démontré le succès entier de l'opération.

Nous avons eu depuis plusieurs témoignages oculaires donnés par des grands blessés britanniques rapatriés.

L'un d'eux venait du camp de Marienbourg où il était infirmier à l'hôpital.

Il a assisté à l'attaque des *Forteresses Volantes* qu'il a décrite en débarquant le 25 octobre dans un port écossais.

"Les avions sont arrivés en file. Quand ils ont survolé l'objectif, ils s'étaient formés en escadrilles de vingt appareils. J'ai compté au moins 96 bombardiers.

"Puis ils ont largué leurs bombes par centaines. Le bombardement n'a duré que deux ou trois minutes. Quand je suis arrivé aux terrains de l'usine, il ne restait que quelques bâtiments, tous endommagés.

"Un officier allemand m'a déclaré qu'il n'avait jamais vu une seule bombe tomber en dehors et je puis ajouter que pas une seule bombe n'est tombée sur le camp de prisonniers français qui se trouve à proximité des usines."

Tous les Britanniques libérés sont d'accord à déclarer que les gardes allemands, jadis brutaux et arrogants, sont maintenant courtois et presque respectueux.

Psychose de novembre

TOUS les indices portent à croire que Goebbels va lancer vers le 9 novembre une campagne destinée à combattre chez les Allemands la hantise de novembre 1918.

Son article dans *Das Reich* du 22 octobre clame : "Nous autres Allemands nous devons démontrer sans relâche qu'une répétition de la débâcle de 1918 est hors de question."

Malgré tout, Goebbels est plus sombre que de coutume. Son slogan est "les gages de la victoire" fait place "aux chances d'une victoire allemande."

Voici un autre passage de cet article :

"Nous ne devons pas être surpris si le destin a rendu les choses plus faciles pour nos ennemis que pour nous. Leur situation est beaucoup plus favorable, car ils possèdent un angle purement matériel, dans le riche réservoir de leurs possessions mondiales (*sic*). Nous autres, par contre, nous devons ménager nos forces et faire le maximum de sacrifice national."

SIEG HEIL !

"Il y a des soucis qui ne peuvent pas être dispersés en sifflotant. Il suffit d'écouter les conversations de nos soldats et officiers pour se rendre compte que tous nos graves problèmes de guerre sont discutés.

"...Chacun doit se rendre compte pleinement, quand il formule des critiques, que ses paroles circulent et peuvent avoir un effet négatif. Un seul être humain par sa conversation suffit pour ébranler la confiance dans la victoire."

Das Reich 23.10.43.

LA LUFTWAFFE EST SURMENÉE

Le Ministère de l'Air annonce que les bombardiers de la R.A.F. en mission sur l'Allemagne ont abattu en septembre 45 chasseurs de nuit allemands.

Un certain nombre ont été endommagés, et il est probable que beaucoup de ceux-ci ne sont pas rentrés à leur base.

Il est à noter que les chasseurs bimoteurs du type *Junkers 88*, *Messerschmitt 110* et *Dornier 217* constituent la principale arme employée contre les bombardiers alliés; cependant les Allemands emploient maintenant de nuit des chasseurs monomoteurs.

Les opérations de la R.A.F. de nuit et de l'Aviation américaine de jour ont obligé l'ennemi à employer tous les appareils qu'il peut réunir, ce qui, évidemment, impose un surmenage à la *Luftwaffe*.

Pacte monétaire hollando-belge

LES gouvernements de la Hollande et de la Belgique ont conclu un accord financier.

Cet accord bi-latéral ne renferme rien qui puisse empêcher les deux pays de donner conjointement leur adhésion à un accord international multi-latéral où ils puissent la participation des autres nations qui adhèrent aux accords monétaires actuellement en vigueur.

En vertu de ce pacte, la Hollande et la Belgique s'engagent à mettre mutuellement à leur disposition leur devise nationale à un taux de change officiel qui sera applicable aux compensations mensuelles prévues.

Il est stipulé qu'il ne sera exigé aucune garantie co-latérale, sous forme d'or ou autre, en ouverture des soldes leur reviendront; il ne sera pas demandé la conversion de ces soldes en or ou en devises étrangères.

Une clause de l'accord délimite le total des soldes créditeurs qu'il sera permis d'accumuler avant de prendre des mesures pour rétablir l'équilibre.

Deux stades sont prévus à ce sujet :

Les soldes créditeurs supérieurs à 500 millions de francs belges ou 30.250.000 florins commenceront à porter intérêt "au taux courant", l'intérêt à la charge du pays débiteur.

Si les soldes atteignent 1 milliard de francs belges ou 60.500.000 florins, il est stipulé que les deux gouvernements se consulteront afin de restaurer l'équilibre.

Dans ce cas, l'accord ne précise pas quelles seront les mesures à prendre pour atteindre cet objectif.

Dans les circonstances actuelles créés par l'occupation de leur pays et d'une large partie de leurs territoires d'outremer, il est évident que les deux gouvernements ne sont pas en mesure de prendre des décisions définitives.

Cependant, l'accord est important puisque, dès la période qui suivra la fin des hostilités, les deux pays auront le moyen de remédier à un déséquilibre dans leurs balances commerciales.

Il vient d'être fait le premier pas vers une mesure plus large de coopération dans le domaine des échanges commerciaux.

Il est de plus significatif que la décision d'effectuer les règlements à porter intérêt ou voie de "clearings" ait été prise par deux membres de l'ancien bloc d'or.

Page 3

LE COURRIER DE L'AIR

AVEC L'ARMÉE DE LA LIBERATION YOUGOSLAVE

Un groupe d'officiers et de soldats britanniques qui combat avec les Chetniks du général Mihailovitch. Faits prisonniers en Crète, ils se sont échappés d'un train qui les menait en Allemagne. (Photo par radio).

23 Octobre

Le 23 octobre 1942, la VIIIe Armée britannique, commandée par le général Montgomery, lui-même sous les ordres du général Alexander, se lançait à l'assaut des positions de Rommel entre El-Alamein et la dépression de Quattara.

Dix jours plus tard, Rommel était en pleine retraite vers l'ouest.

Ainsi était inaugurée la stratégie qui, selon le général Smuts parlant au Guildhall de Londres le 19 octobre 1943, "a rétabli nos communications vitales, conquis des bases essentielles pour l'attaque de la Forteresse hitlérienne, et provoqué la capitulation d'une grande puissance européenne ".

Aujourd'hui, un an après, la Forteresse est entamée, la Méditerranée est une mer alliée, et l'offensive aérienne contre l'Allemagne a été déclenchée à partir des bases italiennes : tel est, en fait, l'actif purement méditerranéen d'une stratégie dont la réussite a fortement influé sur la fortune des armes alliées sur tous les autres théâtres.

Atlantique, où les forces navales et le tonnage libérés de la Méditerranée ont pu aider à écarter la menace sous-marine.

Russie, où quelque 40 divisions allemandes qui remplacent désormais les Italiens en Italie et dans les Balkans, eussent été d'une aide précieuse à l'ennemi.

Offensive aérienne contre l'Allemagne, maintenant prise entre deux feux.

* * *

Alamein fut préparée à Washington, en juin 1942, par MM. Churchill et Roosevelt, alors même que, Tobrouk tombée, l'Allemagne semblait à deux doigts de s'assurer la maîtrise de la Méditerranée.

Depuis lors, une double chaîne d'événements, sur deux plans différents, a conduit les Alliés de victoire en victoire. Première chaîne et mère de la seconde : les consultations successives entre le Président, le Premier Ministre et leurs Etats-Majors ; deuxième chaîne : celle que jalonnent les noms de El-Agheila, Tripoli, Mareth, Akarit, Zaghouan, Tunis, Bizerte, Cutane, Randazzo, Messiane, Salerne, Naples, Bastia (pour ne parler que du théâtre méditerranéen).

Dans son dernier rapport à la Chambre des Communes, M. Churchill a en partie soulevé le voile qui recouvre les grandes conférences interalliées.

En juin 1942 à Washington, a-t-il dit, furent décidées l'offensive contre Rommel et l'opération d'Afrique du Nord. En janvier 1943, à Casablanca, la destruction des armées allemandes en Tunisie, et l'invasion de la Sicile. En 1943, à Washington, " la capitulation de l'Italie cette année ". Sur Québec, qui eut lieu en août, et sur Moscou, qui se poursuit actuellement, nous n'avons, bien entendu, aucun renseignement à donner.

Mais on remarquera que les conférences précédentes s'étaient proposé des buts toujours plus vastes et plus difficiles, et que chacun de ces buts a été atteint en avance sur l'horaire prévu.

Sur le champ de bataille d'El-Alamein, les Alliés prirent la mesure de l'ennemi sur un terrain choisi par eux.

L'expérience de Sicile et de Salerne permit de faire toucher du doigt et de parer aux inconnues redoutables d'une opération amphibie sur une échelle jamais encore envisagée.

A Québec et maintenant à Moscou, c'est donc en toute connaissance de la force réelle et des faiblesses de la Forteresse hitlérienne et des besoins de l'Europe que les Alliés ont délibéré des offensives à venir, et délibèrent de l'avenir de l'Europe et du monde.

La part de la Résistance française dans le débarquement d'Alger

IL Y A UN AN, dans la nuit du 7 au 8 novembre 1942, les Alliés débarquaient à Alger. La première étape de la rentrée dans la guerre de l'Afrique du Nord Française était accomplie.

Aujourd'hui à Alger siège le Comité Français de la Libération Nationale qui, avec les organisations de la Résistance française, dirige l'effort de la France et de son Empire pour la libération de la Métropole.

Quand les forces américaines se présentèrent devant Alger, au lieu d'essuyer le feu des batteries côtières, elles furent accueillies par des signaux, et à terre, au lieu d'être confrontées par la résistance militaire, elles trouvèrent des guides amis qui, avec leurs compatriotes, avaient préparé le terrain en neutralisant d'avance les résistances militaires locales, terrestre et aériennes.

C'est grâce à une série d'organisations de résistance que des patriotes français purent permettre aux Alliés de débarquer sans combat.

L'armistice entraînait quelques jours après en même temps qu'un " Cessez le feu " dans toute l'Afrique française, un acte dont l'avenir immédiat devait révéler non seulement la portée politique, mais aussi l'importance militaire : la rentrée de l'Armée d'Afrique dans la lutte.

Voici comment ont été faits les préparatifs pour libérer Alger, citadelle de la Collaboration, fortifiée par vingt-huit mois de propagande allemande et défendue par onze mille soldats et vingt mille vichystes armés.

A Oran, dès l'armistice, un groupe de jeunes médecins et étudiants avait formé un groupe de résistance.

Puis, le 7 mars 1941, il fut décidé de monter une organisation puissante et de grouper tous les éléments luttant contre Vichy et l'envahisseur. Du 7 mars au jour du débarquement des Alliés, l'organisation de résistance d'Afrique vécut et travailla sans aucune tutelle étrangère.

En août 1941, les premières bases d'une action d'ensemble furent posées à Alger ; en mars 1942, les groupements d'Alger et d'Oran fusionnèrent.

Au début d'octobre 1942, un officier de réserve français reçut l'ordre de prévoir un endroit sûr, où quelques officiers américains pourraient débarquer afin de prendre contact avec des personnalités civiles et militaires françaises.

Pour qu'une pareille opération réussisse, il fallait que les officiers responsables de la surveillance de la côte prissent part activement à l'organisation.

Dans la nuit du 20 au 21 octobre 1942, M. Murphy, Consul des Etats-Unis à Alger, et des chefs de la Résistance s'étaient réunis à la ferme près de l'Oued Messelmoun.

A une heure vingt, un sous-marin guidé par une lumière s'approcha du rivage et fit des signaux. Quatre kayaks, transportant cinq officiers américains et trois officiers de Commando anglais, abordèrent. Pendant la journée du 21 octobre il y eut une conférence entre le général Clark (actuellement Commandant-en-Chef de la Ve Armée américaine en Italie) et le général Mast, chef de la délégation de la Résistance. Les autres personnalités américaines, anglaises et françaises mettaient sur pied les détails du débarquement.

Dans la soirée, l'information parvint que la police avait été alertée et qu'elle se préparait à cerner la ferme et à y faire une perquisition.

Grâce à un stratagème, le Commissaire de Police fut convaincu que dans la ferme ne se trouvait que des Consuls américains qui faisaient la fête. Vers une heure du matin, le sous-marin, appelé par radiophonie, apparut, et après maintes difficultés les Anglais et les Américains parvinrent à monter à bord.

Il s'en était fallu de peu que cette mystérieuse entrevue secrète ne fût découverte et que le secret du débarquement ne fût compromis.

Le succès initial du débarquement du 8 novembre a été assuré par six cents civils, réunis depuis longtemps par des volontaires en face de gens qui ne voulaient pas se battre parce que tous les jours, depuis deux ans, ils avaient la tête martelée par une propagande qui leur vantait les vertus de la défaite.

Pour armement ils disposaient de neuf cents fusils Lebel et de vingt-cinq mille cartouches ; pour les transporter, ils avaient trente voitures touristes et six cars.

Mais, comme l'a écrit un de leurs chefs qui participa à l'opération, leur arme principale c'était qu'ils étaient des volontaires cloisonnés.

Back Page

CHAPTER ELEVEN

FINAL TRAINING

THE END of April 1944 took us to a most unlikely airfield...the Rowley Mile racecourse at Newmarket, and that racecourse was to be pounded with more horsepower in the twelve days that we were there than during most peacetime racing seasons!

At Newmarket I underwent a period of training with another new navigational aid employing a cathode tube display. In this case a radio signal was transmitted from a rotating dish aerial mounted underneath the aircraft. This signal travelled to the terrain below and bounced back to the aerial producing a strong return signal from an irregular ground surface or built up area, but was reflected away by very smooth surfaces or water. I was given instruction on how to operate this new ingenious equipment, which was code named "H_2S".

Flying on a series of exercises in a Sterling bomber over North Norfolk and the Wash I learned to interpret the various signals displayed, and remember vividly seeing the outline of the Wash coast contrasted against the water, together with the very bright and irregular shapes of towns.

I left this secret Radar Training Flight at Newmarket as a qualified H2S Navigator and with promotion to Flight Sergeant.

Our aircrew performance and progress during operational training was recognised with a posting to the Pathfinder School at Warboys, which was commanded by the great air navigator Don Bennett. Instruction was given in special navigation methods and short cuts that would be important for maintaining accurate track and time-keeping. This special training would prove to be invaluable to me later on when doing my job.

We were finally asked whether we wished to continue as pathfinder volunteers as our role would be a dangerous one, but also of vital importance during future operations. All airmen taking the course showed great keenness to carry on as volunteers.

We then moved on to Pershore where we took possession of a brand new Halifax II bomber equipped with the latest navigation aids including, of course, "Gee" and "H2S".

A busy week was spent testing the instruments, radio and radar equipment, as well as swinging and calibrating the compasses for magnetic deviation.   We were delighted with this spanking new aircraft and could not wait to get flying.

Then, it seemed to us, with almost perfect timing, D-Day arrived and we were ready to join the rest of the force into Europe!

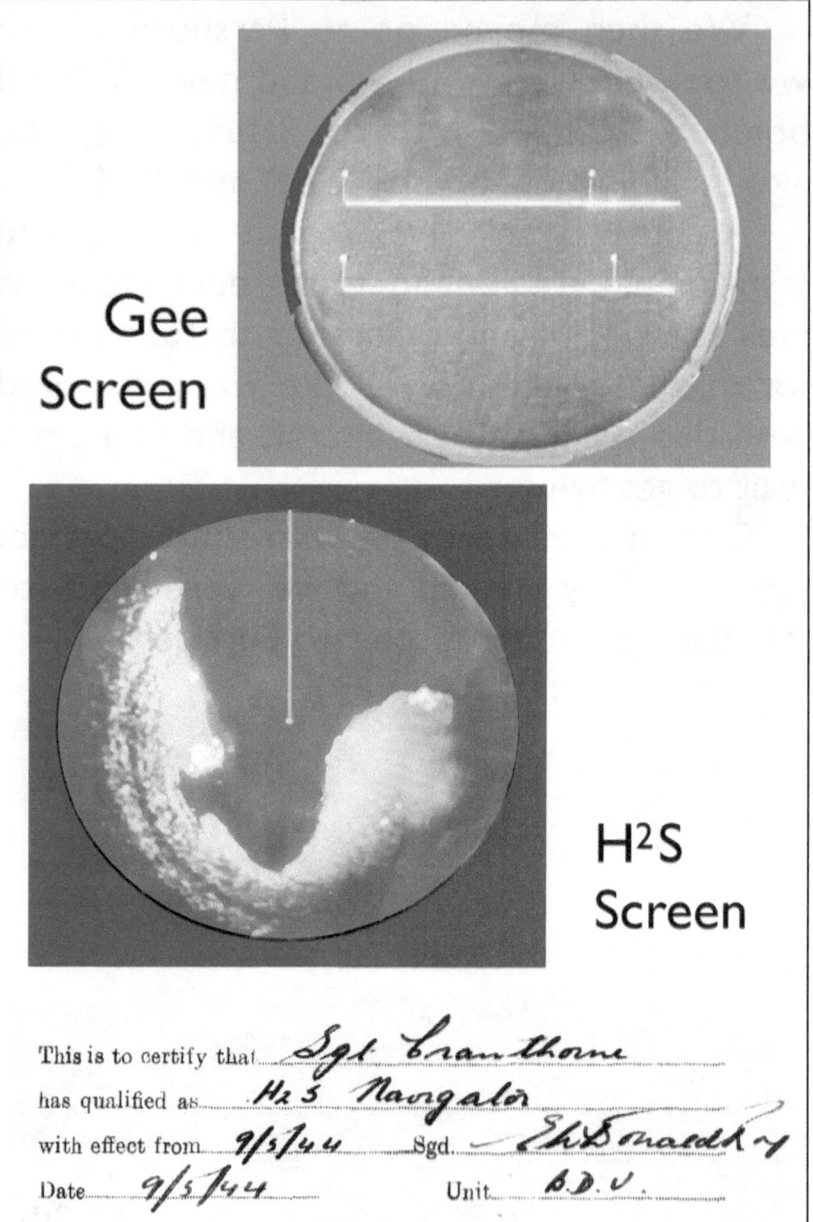

Gee
Screen

H²S
Screen

This is to certify that *Sgt Cranthorne*

has qualified as *H₂S Navigator*

with effect from *9/5/44*   Sgd *Eh DonaldRy*

Date *9/5/44*   Unit *B.D.U.*

We flew back to Rowley Mile at Newmarket for the final checks on our radar systems, and then on to St. Mawgan in Cornwall for some personal medical checks and a final briefing, during which we were told that we would be ferrying our new Halifax, not to France, but to Italy where our forces had already landed in Europe and had reached Rome.

On 16th June 1944, we flew south across the Bay of Biscay, and were acutely aware that our course took us through an area patrolled by enemy fighter aircraft. The accuracy of my navigation was confirmed when, flying parallel to the Portuguese coast, the shore lights were visible. It was reassuring for me to also see an image of the coastline on the H2S screen. After being in the air for nearly six and three-quarter hours, we landed at Rabat Sale, Morocco.

Rabat was hot sunny and dry, and quite a contrast to the pleasant warm days that we had spent at St. Mawgan near Newquay. We eagerly awaited to hear news of where our final destination was likely to be, and it would be a relief to get airborne again.

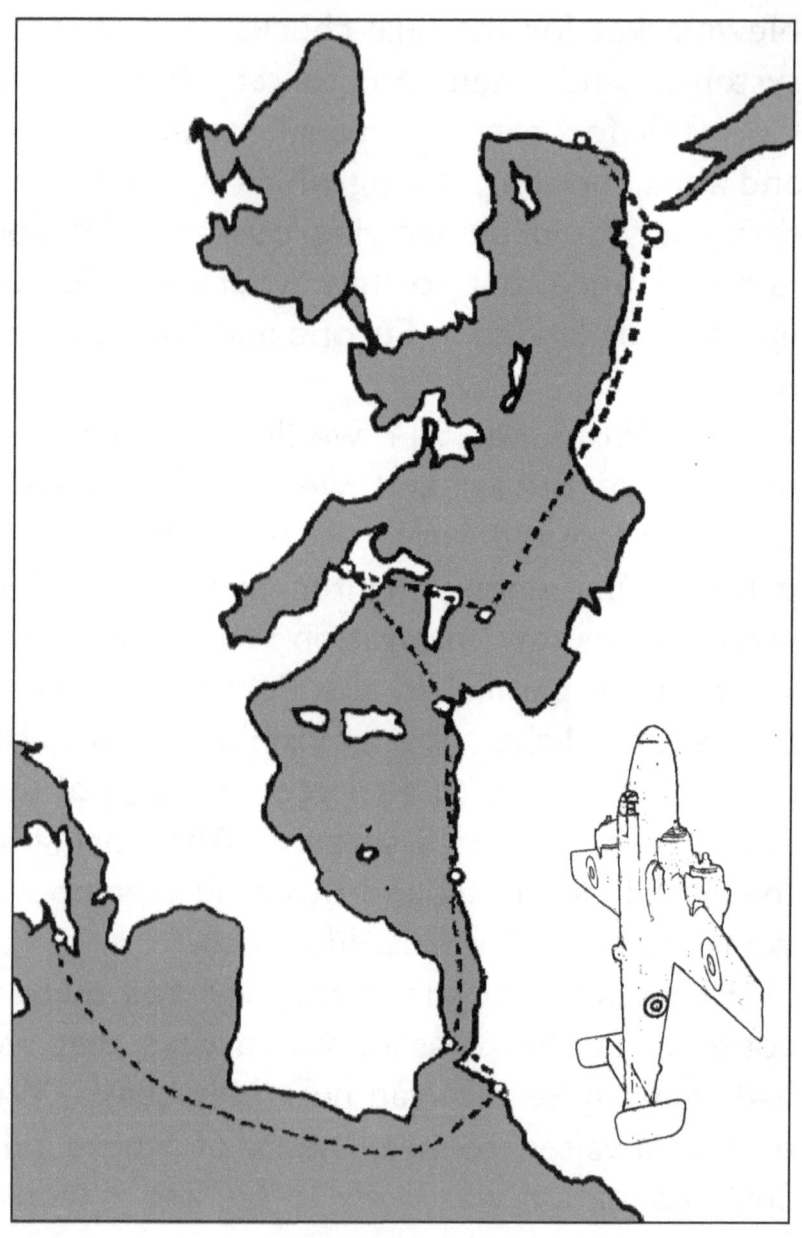

The dry summer heat induced lethargy in the relatively barren surroundings, and little encouragement was needed to adopt the local custom of siesta! Three days later we were airborne and on our way to Gibraltar where the landing skills of our pilot would be tested to the full. Turbulence caused by air currents around the giant rock made for a very bumpy approach as we came down on the runway. This crosses the only road into Spain and the length of the runway is increased by a adding a pier-like extension over the sea, ending in a safety net!

From Gibraltar we flew on to Algiers where we landed at Maison Blanche airport, and were instructed by Flying Control to park our Halifax at a dispersal site where others were already standing. That was the last we saw of our brand new aircraft! Two weeks were spent, under canvas, at Fort le Eau near Algiers where our time was divided between swimming on the local beach, and visits to Algiers, parts of which were decidedly "red light" and very dodgy. Service Police made sure that personnel obeyed Routine Orders making these areas strictly "out of bounds".

RABAT. JUNE 1966

98

FT LE EAU
ALGIERS

JUNE 1944

FT. LE EAU
ALGIERS

99

On July 3rd we boarded a Transport Command D.C.47 and flew as passengers to Bizerte, and then on to Foggia in Italy. At nearby Stonara, we checked in to No. 614 Pathfinder Squadron. It was here that we learned that we would have to take a conversion course to enable us to fly in a Consolidated Liberator which was the main aircraft used on the squadron.

Four days later we boarded a D.C.47 once again, at Bari, and flew on to Malta, Marble Arch (North Africa) and finally landed at Cairo where, at Heliopolis Transit Camp, we awaited our next move.

Prior to our arrival in Cairo, our pilot Les Sims had been experiencing bouts of blurred vision and short blackouts. Following urgent medical checks he was put on the sick list and banned from flying. To our great disappointment we were instructed to leave him behind and proceed by train to Lydda in Palestine.

CHAPTER TWELVE

DROPPING OUR PILOT

AT NO.1675 Heavy Conversion Unit Lydda, Palestine, we were joined by our new pilot, Flt.Lt. John Musgrave, an experienced pilot who had already completed his first tour of operations At Lydda we went through the full routine of circuits and bumps and cross-country flights with bombing practice in our new aircraft, the B24 Liberator four-engined bomber which was mass-produced by Ford Motors in America, and crammed full of electronic equipment and switches. It was being manufactured in great numbers with spares more readily available than for the Halifax. We all had to learn how to manage the new and unfamiliar equipment, a very daunting task for Bill Young, our Flight Engineer.

Johnny Brennan, our rear-gunner, and I, decided to take advantage of our chance of a lifetime and take the Arab bus to visit Holy Places in Jerusalem and Bethlehem.

Our conversion to B24s was completed in seven weeks and we were ready for action! Transport Command carried us back to Italy, where we arrived by truck at No. 178 Squadron, Amendola at dawn on 15th September 1944.

Airfields on the Foggia Plain were constructed across fields where the soil was compacted and raised, then covered with pierced steel planking. Our field was shared with B17 Flying Fortresses; and the Americans, who favoured formation daylight flying, were usually landing at dusk as our Liberators were warming up prior to take-off. "Flying Control" consisted mainly of a caravan parked at the end of the runway from which an Aldis lamp was flashed!

Living conditions, under canvas, could at the best be described as primitive. Heath Robinson would have approved and been overjoyed at the very crude and improvised construction of our "camp beds" the best of which consisted of planking balanced precariously on empty oil drums or boxes.

When it rained, water dripped through the porous roofs of our tents. We were unable to dry our clothing or the unlaundered blankets that had seen service in North Africa. Our issue consisted of two blankets each and during the very cold winter we slept in our flying kit.

A moat dug around each tent hopefully protected the occupants from flooding during the winter rains. In fact winter brought a covering of snow; and a morning shave in freezing water, using an emptied steel helmet, supported by a bomb fin, as a makeshift washbowl, made the sharpest razor feel more like a tenon saw! The Americans were using a new mechanical razor and I promised myself to acquire one after the war.

The food was prepared by smoke blackened cooks using Field Kitchens (fired by oil) and the diet consisted mainly of M.&V. (canned meat and vegetables) with occasionally fried corned beef or Spam. The traditional 'bacon and eggs' was never on the menu for Middle East aircrews!

Dark brown "compo" tea was also in good supply, especially on arrival back at camp following an operation.

FINGER TROUBLE!

We were issued with three pairs of gloves. First there was a pair of white fine silk gloves, then came a pair of brown woolen ones, and finally a pair of leather gauntlets. Even with all three your fingers still got cold but as a navigator I found it impossible to work wearing all three pairs of gloves.

I wore the silk gloves, which enabled me to pick up protractor & pencil and operate equipment reasonably well.

The condensation from my breath dripped from the oxygen mask onto the plotting chart and froze. I worked wearing silk gloves and wrapped my fingers round the small angle poise lamp to try to warm them before quickly putting on the woolen gloves followed by the gauntlets.

Temperature drops 1.75 degrees Celsius per 1,000 feet

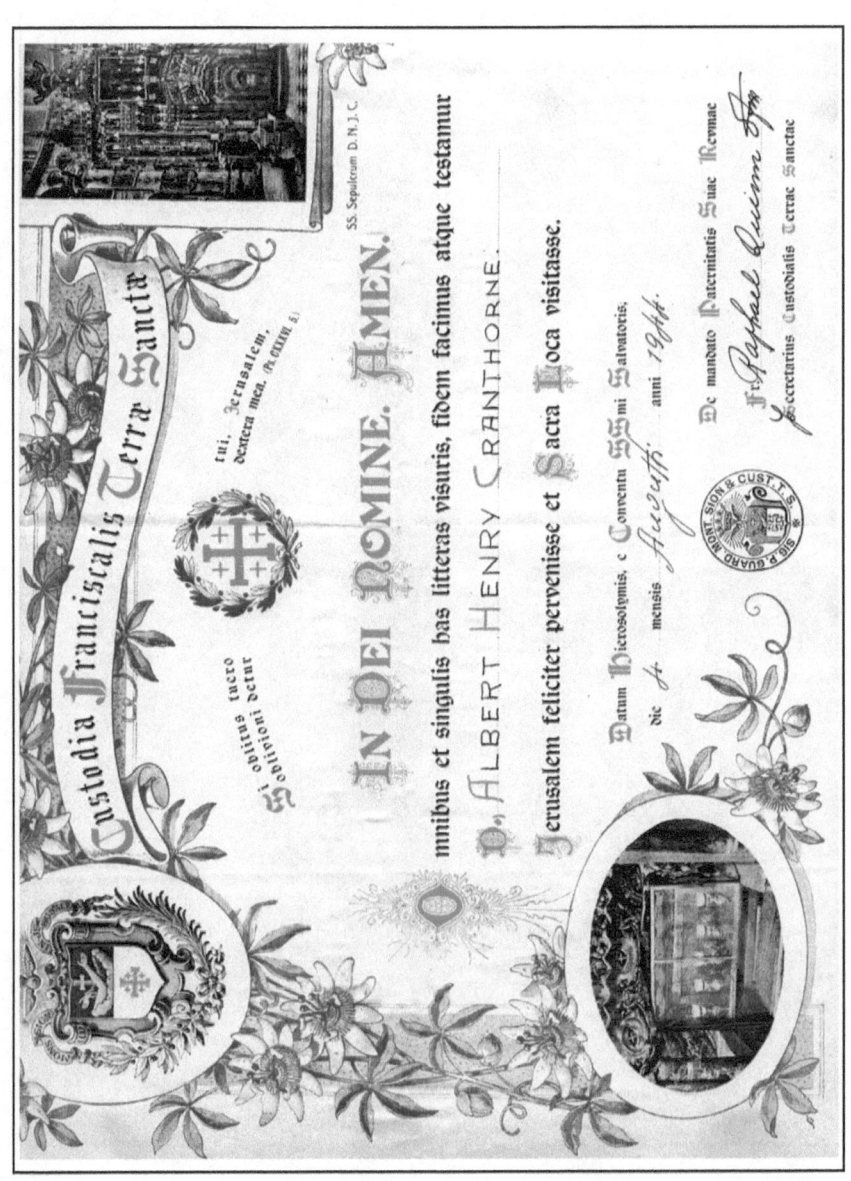

105

A street scene in Bethlehem

the Jaffa Gate to old Jerusalem

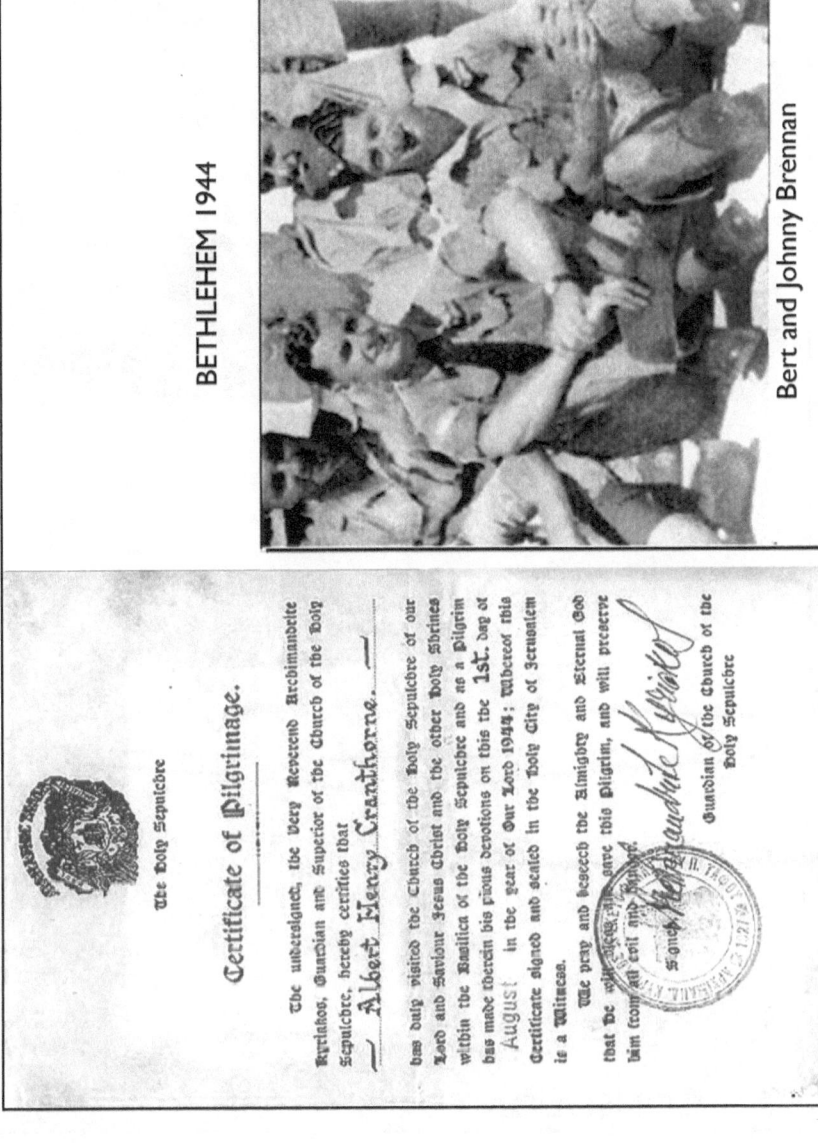

BETHLEHEM 1944

Bert and Johnny Brennan

CONSOLIDATED LIBERATOR B.VI

CONSOLIDATED LIBERATOR B.VI

Type: Long range bomber/reconnaissance

Powerplant: Four 1200hp Pratt & Whitney
                 R-1830-43 Twin Wasp radial
                 engines

Performance: Max speed 290mph
                 Service ceiling 28,000 ft

Weights: Empty 36,500 lb
                 Max loaded 65,000 lb

Dimensions: Span 110 ft
                 Length 66 ft 2 in
                 Height 18 ft
                 Wing area 1048 sq ft

Armament: Browning machine guns 12.7mm
                 Normal bomb load 8800 lbs

The Liberator B.Mk.VI was the RAF designation for the B24J, of which 390 were supplied to the RAF. The total number of Liberators of all variants supplied to the RAF was 1,694.

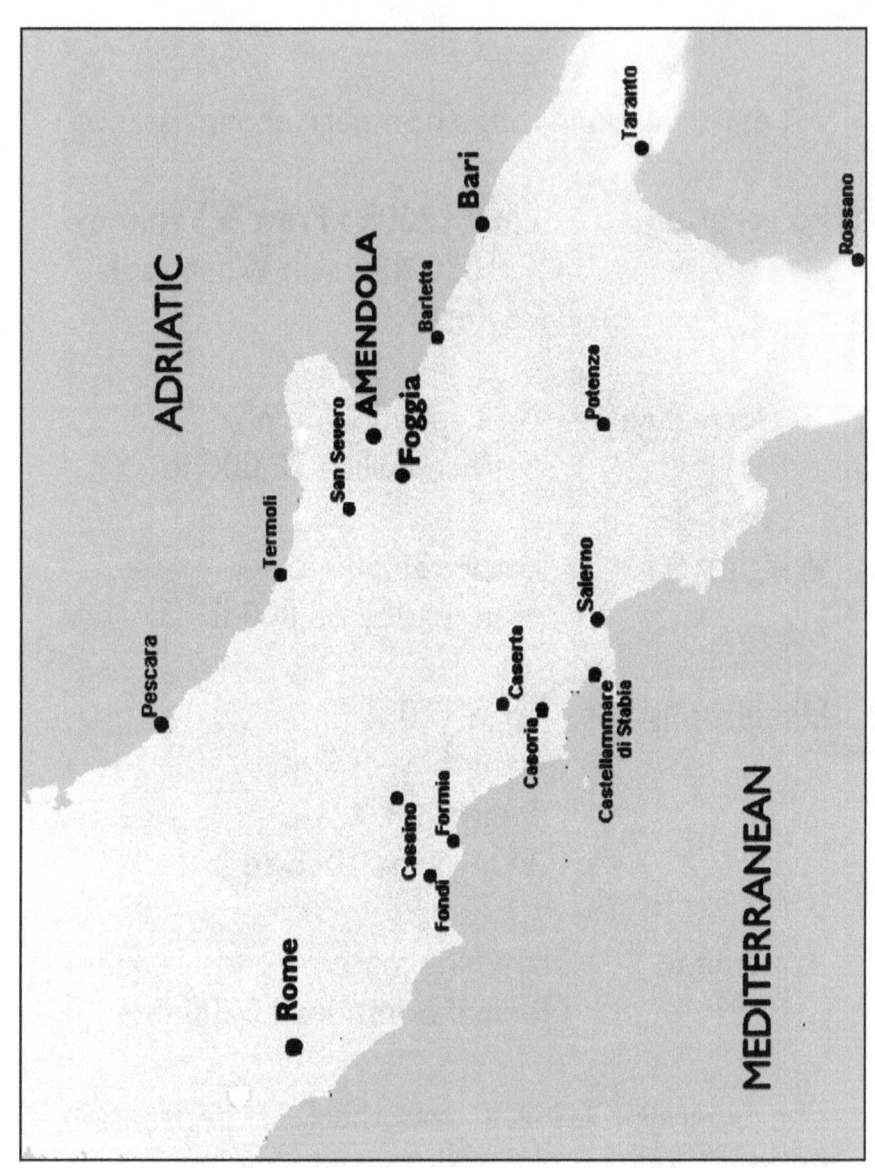

THE ABOVE HAVE ARRIVED.

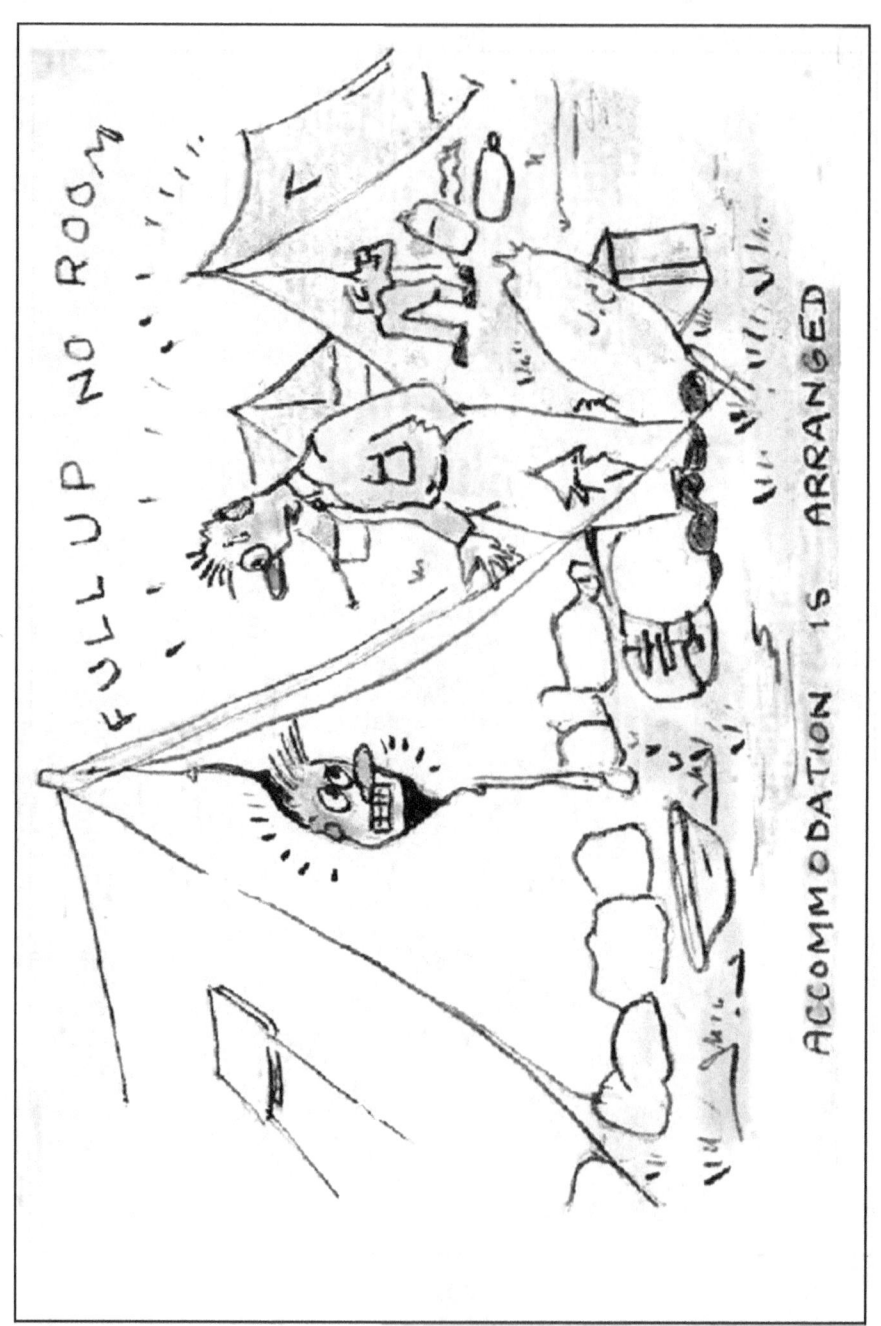

"HE WANTS TO KNOW WHERE TO DRAW A BED!"

113

ALL YOU HAVE TO DO —

IS — PUT UP A TENT —

115

CHAPTER THIRTEEN

178 SQUADRON

178 SQUADRON was formed in Egypt on 15th January 1943 and immediately began attacking targets in Tripoli. It then began operating against targets in North Africa, Sicily, Italy and Crete. With the retreat of the enemy in Tunisia, the Squadron moved near to Benghazi and on 4th March bombed shipping in Naples Harbour. Shipping in Italian and Sicilian ports were bombed during March and April to prevent supplies reaching enemy forces evacuating from North Africa. Targets in Sicily and Italy were heavily bombed prior to the Allied invasion, and the islands of Pantelleria and Lampedusa were quickly captured, and Sicily fell in just 38 days.

Two divisions of the 8th Army crossed the Straits of Messina and landed in Southern Italy in March 1944. The Italians soon surrendered and Italy was occupied immediately by Germany's finest fighting divisions.

The Nazis consolidated their occupation and began a two-year war of attrition in the worst conditions over the most difficult terrain imaginable.

On 1st March 1944 178 Squadron moved to Celone near Foggia and began raids deep into Southern Europe against heavily defended tactical, railway and communications targets including mining of the river Danube at low level.

The Italian port of Genoa received special attention during April. Throughout the summer, in support of the Russian offensive, Hungarian and Romanian rail networks were targeted, as well as those in Austria and Southern Germany, also the vital Romanian oilfields. Water borne traffic on the Danube was reduced by nearly 70% following the raids.

The land campaign in Italy pushed on slowly and relentlessly with fierce and bitter fighting against strong enemy forces, and by D-Day, on 6th June; the 4th and 8th Armies had fought their way as far as Rome and were given a rapturous welcome by the inhabitants of the capital.

In July, 178 Squadron moved to Amendola, near Foggia, and the middle of August saw the start of supply drops to the underground Polish Home Army trapped in Warsaw between the German and Russian armies This required a hazardous round trip of about 1800 miles, and the resultant heavy losses severely depleted the strength of the Squadron.   Operations to Warsaw finally ceased after 11th September, as the Polish uprising had been cruelly crushed.

So it was that we arrived at Amendola on 15th September, in the knowledge that we were part of an attempt to rebuild the depleted Squadron and take part in the Mediterranean Allied Strategic Air Force bombing campaign over occupied Europe.

A.H.Cranthorne

SZEKESFEHERVAR 19 SEP 1944

OPERATIONS RECORD

Date 1944	Aircraft Type & Number	Crew	Duty	Time Up	Time Down
September	Liberator				
18/19th	EW. 276	F/L Musgrave J. R	SZEKESFEHERVAR	18 03	23 45
		Sgt Young W.	Marshalling Yards		
		Sgt Cranthorne A.H.			
		P/O Stedham J. B			
		Sgt Webb A.E.			
		W/O. Deall W.B.			
		Sgt Brennan J.			

2019 hrs R/Yellow TI at position "A". 2039 hrs three batches of flares above target area. 2041 hrs red TI's at target area. 2044 hrs - red TI's at target area - unable to identify target owing to smoke haze. Bombed centre of four red TI's. 2047 hrs, 11,000 ft - all bombs dropped in one stick 100ft spacing on heading 230° IAS 155 mph results not observed owing to smoke haze. Photograph taken. Bombs carried 8 x 1,000 lbs. G.P's .025

OPERATIONS RECORD

Date 1944	Aircraft Type & Number	Crew	Duty	Time	
				Up	Down
October 4th	Liberator EW.276	F/L Musgrave J. R	RIVER DANUBE	19.40	20.20
		Sgt Young W.			
		Sgt Cranthorne A.H.			
		P/O Stedham J. B			
		Sgt Webb A.E.			
		W/O. Deall W.B.			
		Sgt Brennan J.			

Aircraft returned early due to fire in No.2 engine. Bombs jettisoned on land on heading 040°M. between 41°26'N 15°43'E and 41°31'N 15°48'E. Jettisoned safe from 200ft. Flash seen on ground at position 41°38'N 15°32'E.

CHAPTER FOURTEEN

OPERATING

NAVIGATORS attended an early briefing to take note of route details, target information and timings so that maps and charts could be made ready. All-important timings were also given to ensure that bombing and photography were phased over the target. At the main briefing all aircrews assembled to hear the final details including those specific to crew members.

The Intelligence Officer stood in front of a map with small red flags denoting the known position of anti-aircraft guns, and, with eyes aimed at the navigators, usually advised "Go round it eh? - Make a careful note of the flags!" A synoptic chart covered with isobars and symbols was then displayed by the Meteorological Officer who gave his best predictions for the weather, with wind direction and speed over the route and target area. Quite often, at this stage of the proceedings, news was given of a last minute change of route, and the pins and tape were rearranged for noting by navigators!   Trucks ferried us to the airfield, two crews usually filling each truck.   Navigators struggled to hold together maps, instrument bags and sextant hoping that everything would be safely installed in the aircraft ready give the first course to the pilot!

On 19th September we took off on our first operation, which was the bombing of a rail marshalling yard at Szekesfehervar in Hungary.   My memory of this five and three-quarter-hour sortie is dominated by the few minutes over the target area   We arrived at the exact specified time, and I programmed the bombing panel with my latest wind direction and speed figures. Looking down from my position in the nose of the Liberator, I beheld a scene filled with flickering lights of all colours and brilliance, criss-crossed with lines of tracers moving in all directions The whole produced a picture of terrifying fascination. The aircraft camera began rolling; the bombs were dropped followed by the brilliant photoflash, which recorded the position of our bomb bursts.

I gave the course out of the target and we headed back to base.

During take-off fully loaded on our third operation one of our engines exploded and caught fire. We were barely airborne and spent an anxious forty minutes trying to maintain height as Bill Young and our Bomb Aimer struggled to jettison the un-fused bomb-load in fields clear of the airfield. The skill of John Musgrave brought us down safely with wheel brakes smoking as we approached the far end of the runway.

On 12th October our target was the rail marshalling yard at Bronzola in northern Italy where the enemy were bringing supplies through the Brenner Pass. The forecast wind direction and speed provided by the Met. Officer proved to be inaccurate and it was not until we crossed the Italian coastline that I was able to fix our true position and calculate a course to bring us to our final turning point at the southern tip of Lake Garda on time. As we neared Ferrara, I remember warning "Watch out for fireworks!" but we were immediately hit by an anti-aircraft shell which shot away the bomb doors together with six 1000lb. bombs and racks. Bill Young, our Flight Engineer, gave a clear and full account of our damage, in strong colourful language, whilst struggling to fight and extinguish a fire in the bomb bay, with the aircraft dropping in a steep dive to avoid the searchlights. My ground position was accurately confirmed by our encounter and we flew on to Bronzola railway marshalling yards, where we dropped our two remaining bombs on E.T.A.!

As well as attacking many heavily defended targets including Bronzola, Villach, Salonika, Szombathely, Verona, Pola and the railway sidings at Sarajevo we also undertook supply drops to partisan forces in Yugoslavia and northern Italy, where containers were parachuted down at low level in narrow valleys in mountainous terrain on targets marked by flares on the ground in predetermined letters or shapes. On 8th November, near Novi Pazar, the nose was hit by light flak, missing me by a few inches!

OPERATIONS RECORD

Date	Aircraft Type & Number	Crew	Duty	Time	
				Up	Down
October 12/13th 1944	Liberator EW. 276	F/L Musgrave J. R	BRONZOLA MARSHALLING YARDS	17.27	23.00
		Sgt Young W.			
		Sgt Cranthorne A.H.			
		P/O Stedham J. B			
		Sgt Webb A.E.			
		W/O. Deall W.B.			
		Sgt Reynolds R			
		Sgt Brennan J.			

2015 hours - flares over target area. 2017 hours - flares over target area and other flares well North East of target. 2022 hours - green TI's. 1831 hours - S/W at position "A". 1946 hours. SM/W and yellow TI at position "B" Marshalling Yards not definitely identified, but saw bend in river and ware-houses . Bombed visually. 2021 hours , 12,000ft- 2 bombs dropped on heading 140°. IAS 170 mph. Results not seen. Slight H.A.A. at target. Three bomb doors and bombing gear shot away by A.A. near FERRARA 6 bombs blown off when hit.

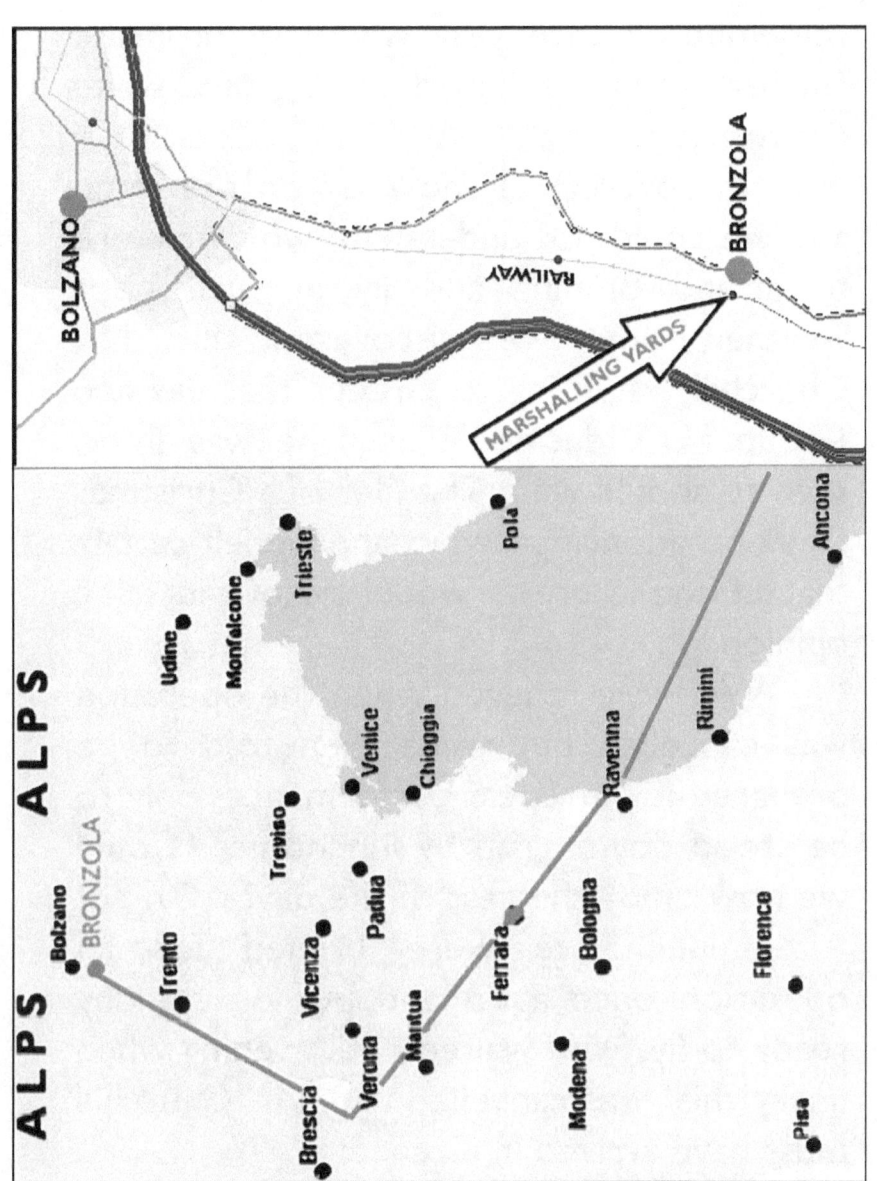

Christmas Day 1944 will always be well remembered each year when we hear the familiar strains of "I'm dreaming of a white Christmas".

A covering of snow lay on the camp and we could not understand why we were to attend Briefing and fly in such poor weather, until we discovered that Mr. Churchill was flying to Greece that day and Group H.Q. decided that if he was flying, then so should we. The idea of a Christmas Day operation appalled us and we felt certain that Luftwaffe crews would be of the same opinion.

We were relieved when the operation was cancelled but were then told to be prepared for a repeat performance; only to be stood down again by lunchtime Could we now enjoy the rest of the day? Oh no! After lunch we were briefed for an operation once again and put on standby ready to fly. We waited until evening when finally this was cancelled too. Mr. Churchill must have arrived in Greece!

Bombing operations and supply dropping (weather permitting) continued into 1945, concentrating on railways, bridges, roads and other communications targets in northern Italy, Austria and Yugoslavia. On 20th March, against the rail junction at Pragersko, an ammunition train was hit and exploded causing considerable damage.

Our final target was the marshalling yard at Villach in Austria. This was a difficult one in a deep valley and extremely sad for us as a Liberator flying dead astern of us developed a fire in the port wing and spiralled to starboard and fell 2-3,000 feet before finally exploding. The crew would have stood little chance of escaping. We discovered later that they were good friends of ours who were also approaching the end of their tour, and were in friendly competition with us to reach a total well in excess of the required 30 operations..

It was a sad and shattering blow to us and also a horrible realisation that such tragic events had become a "way of life". So it was that I ended my first tour of operations with a total of 38.

OPERATIONS RECORD

March	Liberator	S/L Musgrave	J.R.	VILLACH	1805	2155
22 1945	KH 202	F/S Young	W.	MARSHALLING		
		P/O Cranithorne	A.H.	YARDS		
		P/O Stedham	J.B.			
		F/S Webb	A.E.			
		Sgt Reynolds				
		F/S Brennan	J.			
		Sgt Gibson				

1954hrs approximately 46 00N:14 20E – red light on ground – turned green then yellow. Extinguished for a minute then reappeared. Target identified visually. Bombs aimed at centre of red TI's. 2015hrs – 9,500' – all bombs dropped in one stick with 80' spacing on heading 282°. IAS 165mph. Results not seen. Several sticks bursting around and on TI's. Much smoke from bombing. Incendiaries seen near TI to North. Approximately 12 HAA guns firing into stream up to 14,000'. 2015 ½hrs – 9,800' – immediately after bombing, Liberator dead astern, same height. Fire seen to develop on port wing and aircraft spiralled to starboard. Lost 2-3,000' and exploded. No parachutes seen. 2016hrs – 9,800' target area – on run out, red appeared similar to verey light, fired horizontally from ahead. Passed aircraft to starboard, level, no track.

"TRANSPORT 1800 TAKE OFF 1900..."

NAVIGATORS ATTENDED EARLY BRIEFING

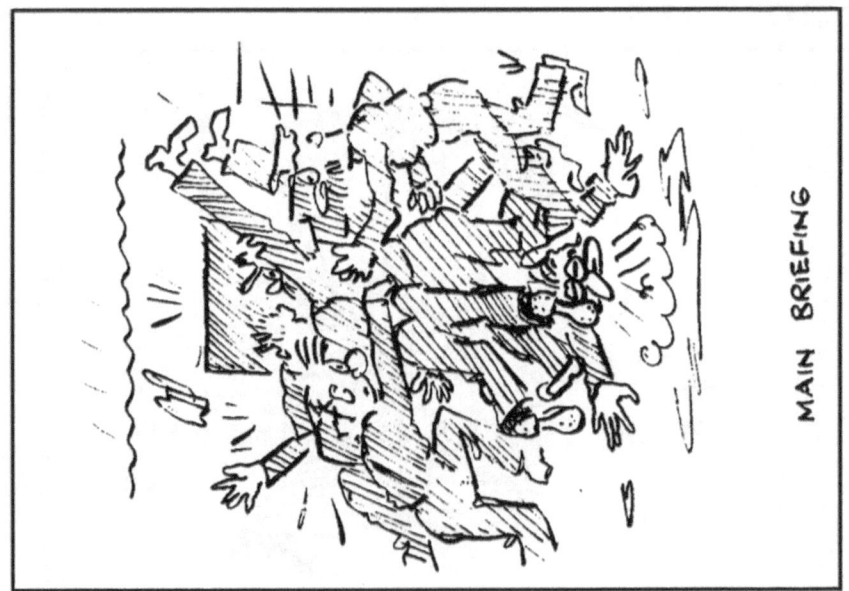

NAVIGATORS STRUGGLED WITH THE LOAD

"TRANSPORT IN FNE MINUTES"

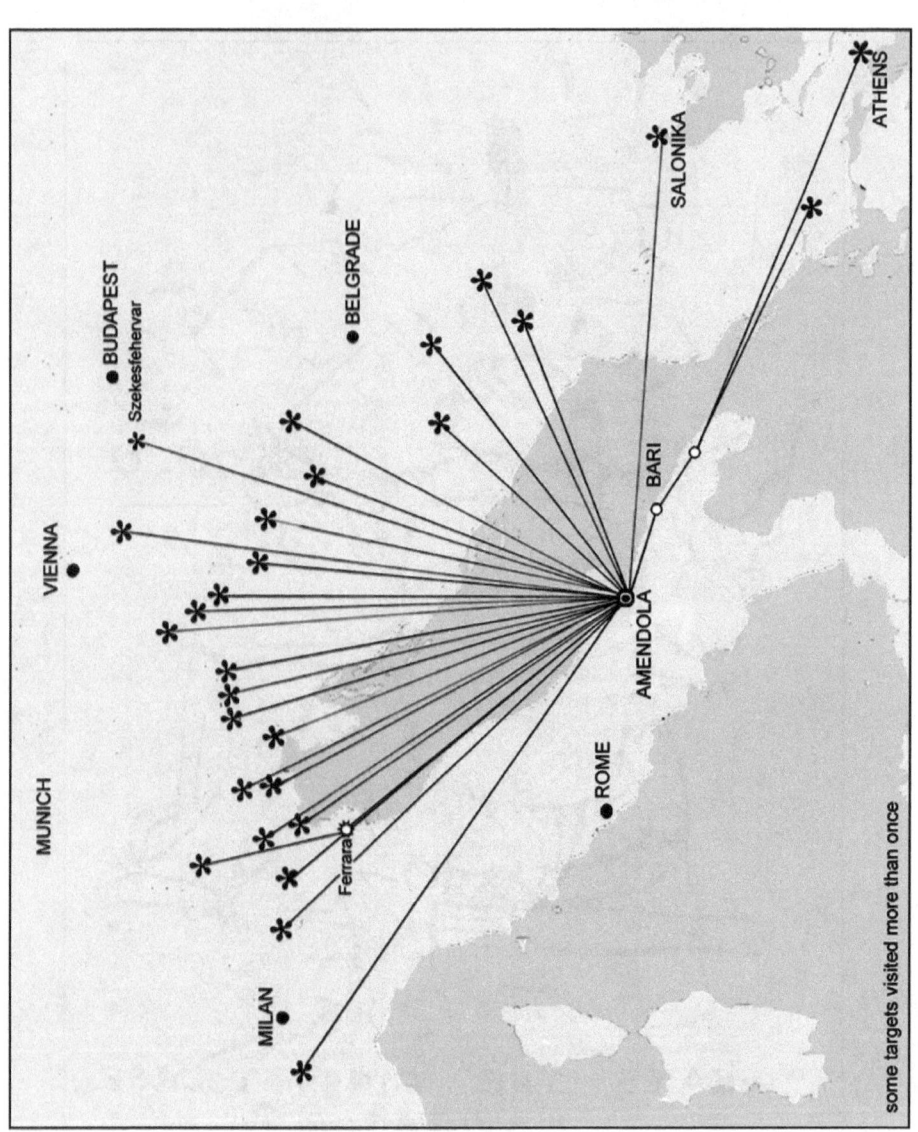

ATHENS

SALONIKA

BUDAPEST
● Szekesfehervar

● BELGRADE

VIENNA
●

BARI

MUNICH

AMENDOLA

ROME
●

Ferrara

MILAN
●

some targets visited more than once

138

SUMMARY FOR Nº 178 SQUADRON

TYPE OF AIRCRAFT. - LIBERATOR VI

TOTAL OPERATIONAL FLYING TIME —— 163.15 HOURS

TOTAL NON-OPNL. FLYING TIME. —— 1.30 HOURS.

TOTAL FLYING TIME —— 164.45 HOURS

TOTAL OPERATIONS. —— 36

SUMMARY FOR FIRST TOUR

TYPES OF AIRCRAFT. - WHITLEY V
HALIFAX II
LIBERATOR VI

TOTAL OPERATIONAL FLYING TIME —— 174.10 HOURS

TOTAL OPERATIONS —— 38

O.C. 'A' FLIGHT 178 SQUADRON.

O.C. Nº178 SQUADRON.

READING ROOM !

Old habits died hard when enloying the "facilities" on 178 Squadron!

W/O W.B.Deall   F/Sgt. J.Brennan   Sgt. A.Reynolds   F/Sgt. W.Young
P/O J.B.Stedham   S/L J..R..Musgrave   P/O A.H.Cranthorne   F/Sgt. A.E.Webb
D.S.O.

JOHN MUSGRAVE

CITATION FOR THE AWARD OF THE D.S.O.

Acting Squadron Leader J R Musgrave, R.A.F.V.R. (Lieutenant, Royal Regiment of Artillery), Number 178 Squadron - Now on his second year of operational duty, Squadron Leader Musgrave has constantly displayed a high standard of skill and devotion to duty. As a flight commander, both in the air and on the ground, he has set a magnificent example to those serving under him. This officer's tour has been marked by his courage and determination to complete his mission undeterred by either enemy opposition or adverse weather. He has attacked heavily defended targets in Salonika, also at Bronzola, Szombathely, Verona and the railway sidings at Sarajevo. On one occasion Squadron Leader Musgrave completed a telling attack on a vital target at a low level, despite appalling weather.

"DINGHY, DINGHY — JOE'S GONE BACK FOR HIS DIVIDERS!"

142

ROME 1945

CAIRO 1945

BRIEFING OFFICER MILAN

R.A.F. FORM 441

SQUADRON _____

CAPTAIN Lt. JOHNSON   A/C NUMBER _____   LETTER K6.6.88   DATE 5.7.45

NAVIGATOR P/O CARRUTHORNE   2nd PILOT

CREW _____

SPECIAL _____

ORDERS _____

SUN		HOON			TWILIGHT	
RISES	SETS	RISES	RISES	SETS	A.M.	P.M.

WATCH _____ AT _____ G.M.T. _____

Det. Slow / Fast _____

FROM TO	W/V USED	HEIGHT FT.	T.A.S	REQ. TRACK (T)	COURSE (T)	VAR.	COURSE (M)	D.R. G/S	DIST.	TIME	STAGE	FORECAST WINDS					
												FROM TO	0 FT FROM T SPEED	5000 FT FROM T SPEED	10,000 T FROM T SPEED	20,000 FT FROM T SPEED	100 FT FROM T SPEED
UDINE KLAGENFURT	3uo/25	18000	176	053	045	3w	048	168	66	23½			3uo 25				
KLAGENFURT GRAZ	347/25	10000	176	060	052	3w	055	170	60	21							
GRAZ A	3uo/25	10000	176	049	0-11	3w	044	165	81	20½							
A B	3uo/25	8000	1185	015	010	3w	013	155	9	3½							
B 6	303/32	8000	176	3u	3u7	3u	316	150	17½	7							
LANZ KLAG	300/25	11000	196	240	246	3u	249	168	60	21							
KLAG UDINE	205/25	11000	186	233	240	3u	243	170	46	23							

WEATHER FORECAST.

CHAPTER FIFTEEN

JOURNEY'S END

HAVING more than completed our required number of operational sorties, a break of six months for training lay ahead of us. An advanced navigation course now attracted my attention and I applied for a place as a student at the Middle-East Staff Navigation School in Palestine.

Travelling as a passenger on a R.A.F. Transport Command Dakota, I arrived at the school at Ein Shemer on 31st March 1945. This meant four and a half months of intensive study, including over 64 hours of air navigational exercises in a Vickers Wellington aircraft, which ended with a night flight from Lydda to Malta, followed by a successful examination and assessment on 17th July.

During my time on the course, the war in Europe ended with the unconditional surrender of Germany on May 7th, with the celebration of VE-Day the following day.

I flew back to Italy via Cairo and reported to 216 Group Headquarters, Caserta, then 249 Wing at Bari for further orders. From there I was posted to Udine in northeast Italy with duties in the Briefing Room of 61 Staging Post, RAF Transport Command.

My next job was senior Briefing Officer at 146 Staging Post, Milan and I was required to close down Transport Command operations there before moving on to Pomigliano near Naples as the Briefing Officer on 12th February 1946. Naples was most memorable for visits made on the back of a lorry to the San Carlo Opera House to see all the main operas, and hear the voices of Beniamino Gigli, Renata Tebaldi and Tito Gobbi.

My Release date arrived and I began the long journey back to England via Austria, southern Germany and France. After crossing from Calais to Dover, our journey continued to the RAF Release Centre at Hednesford where we were quarantined. Finally on 2nd July, I began my leave, and headed for home carrying a large cardboard box filled my new civilian clothes. My effective day of release (last day of service) was 30th September 1946.

Once back home with my mother and father in Eltham, Kent, I had to become accustomed to my new life as a civilian and prepare to resume my duties at the Head Office of the London & North-Eastern Railway Police, who were now back in London and established at King's Cross in much larger accommodation than pre-war with many more staff. It was here that I was soon to meet the lovely Doreen Georgina, who became my wife in 1948.

My war medals arrived by post in a small cardboard box (6cm x 8cm), with the compliments of the Under-Secretary of State for Air. As I opened that little box, I realised that the contents represented seven years of total war horror, combined with unselfish sacrifice, determination, anguish, grief, joy, and great and lasting companionship; but through it all shone the unconquerable power of the unique British sense of humour.

R.A.F. FORM 2520C

OFFICER

ROYAL AIR FORCE

SERVICE AND RELEASE BOOK

Rank .... F/o ....

Personal Number ..... 189652 ....

Surname ..... CRANTHORNE ....

Initials ..... A. H. ....

Class of Release ..... A. ....

Age and Service Group No. ..... 41 ....

---

8. **Queries on Emoluments.**

(i) Any queries on your allowances, or your War Gratuity entitlement, or your Post War Credit arising after you have left the Dispersal Centre are to be addressed to the Accountant Officer of the Dispersal Centre and you are to quote the following particulars:—

(a) Your Class of release (A, B or C.)

(b) The date stamped on the Clearance Certificate in this book.

(iii) Any queries arising from your pay are to be addressed to the appropriate Air Force Agent.

(iii) The final balance of pay received by you does not preclude any adjustment of Income Tax liability which the department of Inland Revenue may require to make subsequent to release.

9. **AUTHORISATION OF RELEASE**

To be completed in Unit except where marked *

Rank ..... F/o ..... Number ..... 189652 .....

Initials ..... A.H. ..... Surname ..... CRANTHORNE .....

(BLOCK LETTERS)

To be completed at the Dispersal Centre. { Release of the above named officer is hereby authorised as a Class ..... A ..... Release.

The effective date of release (i.e. last day of service is ..... 30.9.46. **

Instructions to Class B release to report for employment:

You have been released to take up employment

Delete one of these { as a ....

Industry Group Letters ..... Occupational Classification Number

and are to report within seven days from this date to

the following exchange ....

with Messrs ....

of ....

to whom you are to report within seven days from this date.

You will ordinarily be required to commence work on the expiration of your leave, but you may if you so desire commence at an earlier date.

Date .... **O.C. Personnel Department, Dispersal Centre.

150

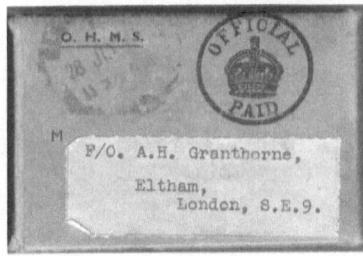

HOME AGAIN

THE LITTLE BOX

SERVICE RECORD

ATTESTATION	11.08.41	B.D.U. Rowley Mile, Newmarket	12.06.44	E
A.C.R.C. St.Johns Wood	10.11.41	ST. MAWGAN	16.06.44	E
A.C.D.W. Brighton	01.01.42	RABAT SALE	18.06.44	E
I.T.W. Torquay	24.01.42	GIBRALTAR	12.06.44	E
E.A.N.S. Eastbourne	12.04.42	ALGIERS Maison Blanche	21.06.44	E
A.C.D.W. Brighton	28.06.42	1 B.P.D. Fort le Eau	21.06.44	K
P.D.C. West Kirby	18.07.42	614 SQUADRON Stonara	03.07.44	K
EMBARK s.s. Volendam	25.07.42	BARI A.T.C.	05.07.44	K
ARRIVE DURBAN	30.08.42	MALTA A.T.C.	09.07.44	K
48 AIR SCHOOL Woodbrook	12.09.42	CAIRO via Marble Arch A.T.C.	09.07.44	K
41 AIR SCHOOL East London	12.11.42 A & B	1675 H.C.U. Lydda	14.07.44	H
CAPETOWN	31.03.43	22 P.T.C. Cairo	04.09.44	
EMBARK Capetown	19.04.43	3 B.P.D. Abu Suer	10,09.44	
HARROGATE	10.05.43	178 SQUADRON Amendola	15.09.44	H
15 E.F.T.S Lake District	10.06.43 C	STAFF NAV. School, Ein Shemer	31.03.45	I & J
HARROGATE	25.06.43	22 P.T.C. Cairo	03.08.45	
2 A.F.U. Millom	03.08.43 A	216 Group H.Q. Italy	23.08.45	K&L
10 O.T.U. Stanton Harcourt	31.08.43 A & D	249 Wing, Bari	26.08.45	
DRIFFIELD	08.12.43	61 Staging Post, Udine A.T.C.	29.08.45	K
1663 CONV. UNIT Rufforth	18.12.43 E F & G	146 Staging Post, Milan A.T.C.	04.11.45	
B.D.U. Rowley Mile, Newmarket	25.04.44 E F & M	POMIGLIANO Naples	12.02.45	
PATHFINDER T.U. Warboys	13.05.44	RELEASE LEAVE	02.07.46	
PERSHORE	19.05.44	Last day of Service	30.09.46	

AIRCRAFT FLOWN IN

LAC	03.04.42		
SGT	26.03.43	OBS/NAV	26.03.43
F/SGT	26.03.44	H2S NAV	09.05.44
P/O	08.12.44		
F/O	08.06.45	STAFF NAV	18.07.45

A - ANSON   G - HALIFAX V
B - OXFORD   H - LIBERATOR VI
C - TIGER MOTH   I - WELLINGTON XIII
D - WHITLEY V   J - WELLINGTON XIV
E - HALIFAX II   K - C47 DAKOTA
F - HALIFAX III   L - C46 COMMANDO
M - STIRLING

Postscript

This collection of memories and drawings is dedicated to the 55,573 bomber aircrew who lost their lives during the war, especially those of whom I knew personally.

Sadly no medal was struck to officially recognise the sacrifice and contribution made by bomber crews.

The ITALY STAR was given for service in that country, but aircrew operating over Europe from Italy did not also receive the AIRCREW EUROPE STAR.